Peter James was educated at Charterhouse, then at film school. He lived in North America for a number of years, working as a screenwriter and film producer before returning to England. His novels, including the *Sunday Times* number one bestselling Roy Grace series, have been translated into thirty-five languages, with worldwide sales of thirteen million copies. Three novels have been filmed. All his books reflect his deep interest in the world of the police, with whom he does in-depth research, as well as his fascination with science, medicine and the paranormal. He has also produced numerous films, including *The Merchant of Venice*, starring Al Pacino, Jeremy Irons and Joseph Fiennes. He divides his time between his homes in Notting Hill, London, and near Brighton in Sussex.

Visit his website at www.peterjames.com
Or follow him on Twitter @peterjamesuk
Or Facebook:
http://www.facebook.com/peterjames.roygrace

By Peter James

DEAD LETTER DROP
ATOM BOMB ANGEL • BILLIONAIRE
POSSESSION • DREAMER
SWEET HEART • TWILIGHT
PROPHECY • ALCHEMIST
HOST • THE TRUTH • DENIAL
FAITH • PERFECT PEOPLE

Children's Novel
GETTING WIRED!

Novella
THE PERFECT MURDER

Short Stories Collection
SHORT SHOCKERS VOLUME ONE

The Roy Grace Series
DEAD SIMPLE
LOOKING GOOD DEAD
NOT DEAD ENOUGH
DEAD MAN'S FOOTSTEPS
DEAD TOMORROW • DEAD LIKE YOU
DEAD MAN'S GRIP • NOT DEAD YET
DEAD MAN'S TIME

The Perfect Murder

(Originally published as part of
the Quick Reads scheme)

Peter James

PAN BOOKS

First published 2010 by Pan Books

This edition published 2014 by Pan Books
an imprint of Pan Macmillan, a division of Macmillan Publishers Limited
Pan Macmillan, 20 New Wharf Road, London N1 9RR
Basingstoke and Oxford
Associated companies throughout the world
www.panmacmillan.com

ISBN 978-1-4472-6603-7

1 3 5 7 9 8 6 4 2

A CIP catalogue record for this book is available from the British Library.

Printed and bound by CPI Group (UK) Ltd, Croydon, CR0 4YY

The 'perfect murder' is the one we never hear about.

Martin Richards QPM,
Chief Constable of Sussex

The Perfect Murder

Chapter One

The idea to murder his wife did not come to Victor Smiley in a sudden flash. Few things *ever* came to Victor Smiley in a sudden flash. He was a man who always planned carefully. He thought everything through one step at a time.

Bit by bit by bit.

In fact, Victor never made any choice until he had carefully worked out every possible option. It used to drive his wife, Joan, bonkers. It drove her almost as bonkers as his snoring. She joked that one day he would have those words, *bit by bit by bit*, on his gravestone. She added that he would probably also die bit by bit by bit.

Victor was forty-two, balding, diabetic, with a comb-over and a pot belly. Joan was forty,

1

plump, with a double chin. When they had first met, Joan thought he was handsome and dashing. Victor had thought she was sex on legs.

They lived in a semi in a quiet part of Brighton. The small house had a view across a built-up valley. They could see the green slopes of the South Downs hills rising on the far side. Most of their time these days, when they were at home together, they were arguing. When they weren't arguing with each other, they argued with their neighbours.

Victor had fallen out with all the neighbours they had ever had. It was one of the many things about him that drove Joan mad. She got mad at him several times a day, most days. Yesterday she was mad at him for buying a television so big it took up half their living room. He was even madder at her for spending a fortune on a new oven. Their old one was quite all right, in his opinion.

Later that evening they had another row, because she wanted to put down a new kitchen floor. He was happy with the one they had. There were years of life left in it, he told her.

2

Then, during the night, they had yet another row. This time it was because of his snoring. In the early days, Victor never used to snore. Now, almost every night she would wake him to tell him he was snoring. It was like sleeping with a sodding elephant, she'd say. More and more often she would have to go into the spare room, just to get some sleep. She would drag herself out of their bed, wrap herself in a blanket and crawl onto the hard single bed in there.

They'd met at a jive dancing class at a church hall in Brighton when Victor was twenty-one. He was doing a course in computers at Brighton Tech and living with his widowed mother. Joan was working as a dispatch operator for a taxi company, and lived with her parents. A friend told Victor that dance classes were a great place to meet 'tottie'. A girlfriend told Joan that dance classes were a great place to meet suitable men.

Victor had seemed very suitable, if a little shy, and clumsy on the dance floor. 'Two left feet, you've got!' Joan teased him when he went over and chose her as his dance partner for the next set. *Great tits you've got, and a stonking pair of legs*, he thought to himself as he struggled to keep his stiffy from nudging into her.

Joan thought he was funny, and sweet, and *very* handsome. He seemed to have a bit of a spark about him. In her view, he was a man who would go places. She ignored the opinion of her parents. Her father thought Victor looked lazy, and her mother said he had *greedy* eyes.

Victor thought Joan was the loveliest creature he had ever set eyes on. She looked like a Page Three girl. When he was a teenager he used to stick photos of Page Three girls on his bedroom wall and lust over them. Of course, he assessed that she had child-bearing hips. He couldn't believe his luck when she agreed to go on a date with him. Then later, when he met her parents for the first time, he studied her mother carefully. He had read somewhere that women always take after their mothers. Well, cor, wow! Well into her late forties, Joan's mother was, in his view, still highly fanciable. So .no worries there. Mother and daughter ticked all the boxes.

On their wedding day, Joan imagined that in twenty years' time Victor would be a high-powered businessman. She thought that they would have four children, two boys and two girls. They would live in a grand house with a swimming pool. Victor imagined that in twenty years' time Joan would still be slim and gorgeous and they would still be having wild sex twice a day. He thought kids would be nice, so long as they did not interfere with their life too much, especially their sex life!

Instead, Victor was stuck in a dead-end job, and they were stuck in the same modest house they had been in for nineteen years, and no children had come along. They lived alone with their ginger cat, Gregory. The cat did not like either of them.

Joan did not like to face the reality that life might always be like this. They would both be unhappy. What kind of future would this be?

They disagreed on just about everything. They even argued most nights on whether to have the bedroom window open or shut. Victor said he could not sleep in a room that was stuffy. Joan said she couldn't sleep in a room where the air was cold.

The worst thing of all for her was when they went to a restaurant. Going out on Saturday nights had long been a ritual for them, and Joan dreaded these evenings more and more. She always made sure they went with another couple, so they didn't just sit and bicker at each other. However, these evenings always turned into slanging matches between Victor and Joan so, over the years, their friends dropped away. All except for Ted and Madge, who didn't have any other friends themselves.

At every restaurant, Victor would spend several long minutes reading the menu, then he would ask the waiter to explain each item in detail. After that he normally asked for something that was not listed. It was almost always the same thing each time: prawn cocktail followed by steak and chips. That was all he really liked to eat. Even if they went for Chinese, which Joan and Madge were keen on, or Indian, which Ted liked even more, Victor would still order his sodding prawn cocktail followed by steak and chips. He would make racist remarks under his breath if they couldn't do it.

'Got to have things you can't get at home!' he would say loudly. Then, with a wink at Ted, and nudging Madge with his elbow, he would add, 'Shame they don't have blow jobs on the menu, because I can't get one of those at home, either!'

Ted would guffaw and rub Madge's thigh under the table. 'We don't have that problem, do we, love?' he would say.

Madge would go bright red and say proudly, 'He's a randy sod, is my Ted!'

Joan would go bright red and apologize to the waiter. She would have liked to add, *I'm sorry I am here with this fat, balding, smug little man with his horrible comb-over, and his loud suit and nasty tie. He was actually thin and quite handsome when I married him!* Of course, she never dared.

Instead, she would hiss at her husband, 'Why can't you try something else for a change? Be bold for once!'

'Because that's what I like,' Victor would always reply. 'Why risk having something I won't like? I could be dead tomorrow.'

Oh God, yes please! Joan would think to herself, more and more often.

It was the same for Victor with books and with television. He only ever read detective stories, and only ever watched detective shows. Sherlock Holmes was his favourite. He had read every Sherlock Holmes story several times. He had seen every film and TV adaptation of his hero. Basil Rathbone was his favourite Sherlock Holmes actor. In Victor Smiley's view, Basil Rathbone was *The Man*.

Victor had strong views on everything, including driving. He would never talk and drive at the same time because, as he would tell Joan over and over, that was dangerous. 'Slow down!' she would tell him all the time when he drove. 'Shut up, woman!' he would reply. 'How do you expect me to drive with you talking? *That's* what's dangerous!'

Victor smoked cigars at home, but for some reason he did not consider smoking cigars dangerous. 'Cigarettes, yes, but not cigars!' he would state. He didn't worry when Joan told him cigars made his breath smell like a dragon's. In the early years, when they were in love, that had not mattered to her. She used to tell him then that he was a horny creature, and that she loved his smoky breath. In later years, it was worse on Sunday mornings when he had not shaved since Friday. She said it was like making love to a fire-eating porcupine.

As for Victor, none of the pretty girls in Brighton's Kitten Parlour ever complained about his breath. They were more than happy to give him all the blow jobs he could ever want. They would also tie him up and spank him, and tell him over and over he was a naughty, naughty boy.

After each visit to the Parlour he would arrive home and crawl into bed beside his sleeping wife (who was putting on weight by the day), and read more detective stories. He would think about the websites on poisons he had visited during the day, and he would go to sleep every night dreaming of a happy future.

Victor's first job had been with a firm near Brighton that made paints for the car repair industry. Cyanide, a deadly poison, was one of the chemicals that were used in this process. One night, when he was working late, he had stolen a bottle of cyanide. For years he kept it hidden among the cans of weed-killer and other bits and pieces in his garden shed.

Recently, as he got more and more fed up with Joan, he would sit in his shed and stare at that bottle. He would dream of using it on her.

So it was that the idea to murder his wife evolved not over days, not over weeks, not even over months, but over a couple of years. However, there was something he did not know. During those same two years, Joan had begun planning to murder *him*.

Chapter Two

The signs had all been there, if Victor had cared to notice. They were stacking up, bit by bit by bit.

Their marriage had started to turn sour when Joan failed to produce a child. They tried for some years, and that part of it had been fun. Then they started on a round of seeing doctors. The problem, they were told, was that Victor had a low sperm count and Joan had hostile mucus. Each blamed the other. Joan taunted Victor that he wasn't really a man. She sneered that real men had dicks that worked properly. He taunted her back, telling her that *real* women did not need sixty-five million sperms because one would be enough.

They made love less and less often until they finally stopped making love at all, except on

Sunday mornings, and then not every week.

Victor looked for relief at the Kitten Parlour. Joan found a lover. When her lover wasn't around, she binged on chocolate and cream cakes. Sometimes she got drunk on *Special Offer* white wine that she brought home from work.

The first clue Victor might have picked up about Joan having a new man in her life was her new hairstyle. At first, he didn't even notice when she changed her hairstyle. Since she'd started putting on weight, he'd started looking at her less.

He was sitting in front of the telly, beer can in his hand, with the cat looking at him sourly from across the room. He was watching Miss Marple in *Murder at the Vicarage*. Joan came in and sat down. She was reading one of the trashy romantic novels she liked. For a good half-hour, Victor thought there was something different about his wife's appearance, but could not put a finger on what it was.

Then it clicked! Her long brown hair, which she had worn at the same length and in the same style since their wedding nineteen years ago, had gone. It was cut short in a modern, razored style. Victor told her she looked butch. Joan replied that he was out of touch, that this was the modern fashion.

The second clue, which he also missed (until he got the credit card statement at the end of the month), was that she started buying new underwear. It was expensive, silky underwear. Then she started buying all kinds of new clothes. He began spotting the items every month on their credit card statement. Or, more correctly, *his* credit card statement, as it was all paid for with *his* money. Her part-time job at a supermarket checkout till didn't pay a lot. He moaned at her about her spending. She replied that she had decided to work for charities, because she needed to put something back into the world. She needed to look smart for the meetings, she told him.

There were endless meetings, night after night. Doing good for the world, she told him. Helping deprived people. It meant that more and more often she stayed out late. She left him with ready meals to stick in the micro-wave, while he watched his detective shows and his sport. That suited him fine. What did not suit him fine were the bills.

She was spending more than he earned, and he had to dip into his savings. That was not his long-term plan at all. He had in mind something far better to do with his savings than buy Joan new clothes. Far, far better!

Joan told him it was good for a couple to have separate interests. She petted his head lovingly, told him he could enjoy his television shows while she went out to help save the world.

At first it all worked well. Apart from her spending. Victor was the IT manager at Stanley Smith & Sons, the ninth-largest makers of egg boxes in England. Now that Joan was busy in the evenings, he could leave the office and go to the Font and Firkin for a couple of leisurely pints of Harveys. He could step outside with the other smokers, and puff and chat away to his heart's content.

Twice a week, when he was drunk enough not to feel shy, he would pop along to the Kitten Parlour just off Silwood Street for a bit of rumpy-pumpy. Then he would head home.

While waiting for the ping of the microwave he would check his blood sugar level and give himself his evening jab of insulin. He would watch a rerun of *Morse*, or a *Poirot*, and feel content.

There was one special girl at the Kitten Parlour he was growing sweet on. Her name was Kamila. She had a tangle of blonde hair and a slender body. She told him she had run away to Brighton to escape from her boyfriend, Kaspar, who beat her up. In the tiny room with the pink bedspread and the price list on the wall (hand jobs, blow jobs, full sex, kissing extra), and the porno movies playing on the little square television, he listened to her tales. One night, as he lay next to her after their ten minutes of rumpy-pumpy, he told her he would like to help her.

Kamila told Victor she liked him. He made her feel safe, and she liked the way he was so manly. That made him feel good. Joan never told him he was manly.

He wanted to give Kamila more money, to help her start a new life in Brighton. He wanted to keep her safe from her bully boyfriend, Kaspar.

He planned a new life for Kamila, with himself.

Before Kamila started on each blow job, she told him that a new life with him would be her idea of paradise. So each time he gave her a bigger and bigger tip afterwards.

That was making his money worries even worse. He was already stretched to keep up the mortgage payments on the house. His overdraft was going up because of the housekeeping money Joan demanded. She was spending so much these days on sexy underwear and new clothes and her fancy hairdresser. It had been all right until recently because his bank manager had been helpful to him. He had been helpful ever since Victor had bumped into him one day in the Kitten Parlour. Now he had left, and the new manager told him he was sorry but, with the credit crunch, that was it. No more money.

The choice came to this: fewer visits to the Kitten Parlour and no more big tips for Kamila. Or, stop Joan spending money.

It was a no-brainer.

He cancelled their joint credit card without

telling her. That night she came home and shouted at him, telling him the card had been declined in Boots and she had never been so embarrassed in her life. She called him a big, fat, lazy turd. She told him her dad and mum had been right and she should have listened to them!

Victor ignored her ranting. He was watching Agatha Christie's *Sparkling Cyanide* on television. He wondered what it would be like to give Joan a glass of cyanide. To watch her collapse and die on the floor in agony, the way the actress on television was doing now.

Little did he know that Joan was thinking exactly the same thing. About him.

Chapter Three

Don Baxter drove a taxi, so his wife never knew where he was. That was just as well, as much of the time these past months Don had been in bed, screwing Joan. He screwed her during the day and, often, at night too. They met in a small flat in Brighton that belonged to a mate who was working on an oil rig in the Emirates.

He made Joan feel young again.

Don's wife had gone off sex after their second daughter was born. That was twelve years ago. With Joan, he'd made up for lost time. He reckoned he'd now had twelve years' worth of sex with her in the past three months. He couldn't get enough of Joan, and nor could she get enough of him. He *liked* her plump body. He liked her big boobs. He told her he liked that she was *ripe*.

Don was a big man, in *every* way. Joan used to smirk, thinking about him when she was lying in bed next to Victor. She would dream of tomorrow and being with him again. Don had been a boxer, then a bricklayer, before becoming a cabbie. He worked out, pumping iron, keeping his six-pack stomach tight and his biceps hard. Not the only part of him that was hard, she thought wickedly.

Don had never met Victor, but he never missed a chance to say something bad about him. The worst thing was the way Victor earned his money. He hated cruelty to animals. Don told Joan that the company Victor worked for made egg boxes for the battery chicken industry. Battery chicken farming was immoral, he said, and that made Victor a bad man.

Joan loved so much about Don. She admired that he had moral principles. This was something Victor lacked. She loved that Don thought outside the box. The egg box!

Don liked his booze and one night Joan came home a little drunk. She told Victor it was disgusting that he made his living out of supplying a trade that was cruel to animals. She demanded to know what he was going to do about it.

'I am not the moral keeper of the nation,' Victor replied. 'If I stopped, someone else would make them.' Besides, he went on to tell her, people were losing their jobs all over the country at the moment, with all the cutbacks. This was not a good time to start looking for new work.

As her love for Don grew, Joan began to hate weekends more and more, especially Sundays. She knew Don was at home with his wife and kids, while she was stuck at home alone with Victor. She couldn't find a way to make the weekends pass faster, but she did at least find a way to really irritate Victor! She bought the DVD of the film *Chicken Run*, about a hen that escaped from a brutal battery farm. She would interrupt Victor's detective show or football game, and play it on the TV.

Each time she played it, Victor got more angry.

So she played it more and more.

Chapter Four

These past couple of years, Victor had hated Sundays every bit as much as Joan did, because it meant he could not see Kamila. He would spend some of the day pottering around in the garden, or with his vegetables in the greenhouse. Or he would sit in his shed, staring at his dusty bottle of cyanide. Killing time. In his mind, he was killing Joan. For him, the only good thing about Sundays was that at least he had Mondays to look forward to.

On this particular Monday morning, in February, Victor got up as usual at half past six. Joan was still asleep. He showered and shaved, humming *The Dam Busters* tune to himself. The theme from the old war film was his favourite piece of music, and he always hummed it when he was in a good mood.

On Monday mornings, these days, he was always in a good mood.

He carefully applied roll-on on his arm-pits and sprayed cologne all over his flabby white body. He adjusted his comb-over, and put on fresh underpants, his best suit and smartest tie.

He knew that for some reason *The Dam Busters* always annoyed Joan more than any other tune. This made him hum it even more loudly as he brought her a cup of tea in bed and switched on the television for her. Then he told her she would have to cut down. No more spending. They had to make ends meet. He left for work before Joan was awake enough to argue back. He was still humming.

The Stanley Smith factory was a two-storey building on an industrial estate in the north of Brighton. Victor greeted a few of his colleagues when he arrived, then poured himself a coffee and stole a biscuit from a packet someone had left out. He trotted along happily to his little office.

Alone in there, quietly and without Joan's

knowledge, he used some of the last of his savings to buy a life insurance policy for her. It would produce a nice cash sum on her death. Enough to pay off his debts, with plenty left over for a new life.

A very nice new life indeed, with Kamila!

Although Victor Smiley's business card said 'IT Manager', that was a grander title than the job deserved. He was the costings clerk and the payroll clerk. He produced the monthly accounts. Much of the time he didn't actually have anything to do at all. Most of the egg box production was done by machines. Most of the people who worked for the company were here to look after those machines. No one noticed that he had plenty of spare time in his job, because he was always careful to look busy.

Of course, Victor Smiley really was very busy indeed. He was spending most of his days learning about stuff on the Internet. Stuff that was connected to his plans. Stuff like case histories of frauds on life insurance companies.

It quickly became clear to Victor that life insurance companies were not stupid. If a husband took out a big policy on his wife, and his wife died a few weeks later, the insurance company would investigate. Most people who had tried that kind of scam ended up on trial for murder.

Victor realized it would be smart to wait, however hard that might be. He would have to be patient. He decided that he would wait a year before killing Joan. Kamila was going to have to be patient too. The big plus was that this would give him plenty of time to think and plan.

One whole year to plan the perfect murder.

So every day, after he had dealt with any urgent business to do with his job, Victor would search websites, typing the words *perfect murder* into Google.

Then he moved on and began Googling *poisons*.

Then, *detecting poisons*.

Everything he wanted was right there, normally just one click of his mouse away. He made careful notes, building up a file. Finally, he had a long list of rules that needed to be kept, to commit a perfect murder. There were fifty-two rules in all. These were some of them:

Rule One: Don't have a criminal record.
Rule Two: Don't have a motive that is clear for all to see.
Rule Three: Plan carefully.
Rule Four: Bloodstains are hard to remove completely. Avoid.
Rule Five: Poisons can be found in post-mortems. Avoid.
Rule Six: Suffocation with a plastic bag is clean and quick. No mess.
Rule Seven: Get rid of the body.
Rule Eight: Don't tell anyone. Ever!
Rule Nine: Remember that thousands of people go missing every year.
Rule Ten: Be ready to deny anything. No body, no proof.
Rule Eleven: Act as if you are missing her.
Rule Twelve: Don't appear with your new lover too quickly after the murder.

Victor was eagerly looking forward to ticking each box when the time came. The plan was taking shape nicely inside his head. He began to write it down, bit by bit by bit. Each time he read it over he hummed proudly to himself. It was a good plan. Genius!

He named it *Plan A*.

Then one day, without any warning, his boss came into his office. His boss was the son of the founder of the Stanley Smith factory. He was the *& Son* of Stanley Smith & Son. Rodney Smith was a big, unpleasant tosser, who drove a gold Porsche. According to office gossip he was screwing his secretary. Smith told him that he was sorry but sales were down, costs were up, savings had to be found. Victor would have to go. He was being made redundant.

He would get severance pay based on the time he had worked for the company. He would get one and a half weeks' pay for each of the sixteen years he had served. That worked out at six months' pay.

Victor was so shocked that after work he drank five pints at the Font and Firkin, as well as four whisky chasers. He had intended to keep the news a secret from Joan but, arriving home blind drunk, he blurted it out.

That night, Joan screamed at him in rage, and told him how useless he was.

At his desk the next morning, Victor had a bad hangover. He worked out how many visits to the Kitten Parlour he could make with six months' pay and the remains of his savings. He realized it would be a lot more visits, and more tips for Kamila, if he did not have to pay housekeeping money.

To save his money, Joan was going to have to go more quickly than he had planned. There was no option. There simply was not enough time for Plan A. He was going to have to go with Plan B.

The only problem was, he didn't yet have a Plan B.

But Joan did.

Chapter Five

The solution came to Victor that night.

As happened most nights now, he was woken at about 2 a.m. by Joan hitting him on the chest and hissing, 'Stop snoring!'

At 4 a.m. Joan woke him again, climbing out of bed and saying, 'God, Victor, you are worse than ever! What do you keep up your nose and down your throat? Trumpets?'

He mumbled a sleepy apology. He heard her leave the room and slam the bedroom door behind her. Then he heard the slam of the door to the spare bedroom. All of a sudden, he was wide awake with excitement. He had an idea.

Joan was always moaning about the little spare room where she went to sleep when his snoring kept her awake at night. It was grotty, she said, and she was right. The walls were the colour of sludge and the thin curtains had moth holes in them. It was the one room they had never bothered to do up after they bought the house. To begin with, they had planned it to be their first child's bedroom. But they'd had no children, of course. So it still had the old single bed which the previous owners of the house had left behind. It was a sad little room.

Every few weeks, Joan would have a go at Victor about it, telling him it was high time to do up the room. She said he should make it look nice in case they ever had an overnight guest. He could at least make it nice for her to sleep in when she couldn't stay in their room because of his snoring. This had been going on for years and years.

Now he thought he had the answer to two problems at once! Making the room nice for Joan, and giving him his Plan B!

Unable to sleep any more he put on his dressing gown and went into the kitchen. Quietly, not wanting to wake Joan, he made himself a cup of tea. He was so excited. Then he went up to his den, switched on his computer and logged on to the Internet. He entered the word *cyanide* into Google.

As he had found before, there were hundreds and hundreds of web pages on cyanide poison. Tonight, he steadily narrowed down his search. He typed in *cyanide vapour*. Then *cyanide gas*. He read every word, greedily lapping it all up. The more he read, the more excited he became. Some things he read over several times because it was better to remember things than to write them down. That was Rule 52: *Leave no tracks*.

This is what he remembered:

The extent of poisoning caused by cyanide depends on the amount of cyanide a person is exposed to.
Breathing cyanide gas causes the most harm.
Cyanide gas is most dangerous in enclosed places where the gas will be trapped.
To some people cyanide smells like bitter almonds.
Cyanide is present in some paints, such as Prussian blue.

Now he *really* smiled. Prussian blue had long been one of Joan's favourite colours.

Chapter Six

Joan wondered what had come over Victor. That weekend, he didn't watch his detective shows or potter around in his shed or his greenhouse. He spent the whole of Saturday and Sunday in the spare bedroom. He was busily decorating it for her.

'For you, my angel!' he told her. 'You are quite right. This room has been in an awful state for far too long. Now I'm going to make it beautiful for you.'

He would not let her in while he was at work. He wanted to surprise his angel, he told her. She could not go in until it was finished!

Every now and then he came out coughing and spluttering. He had a breathing mask pushed up onto his forehead, and wore a white, hooded, paint-spattered boiler suit. It reminded her of the paper suits that she saw Scene of Crime Officers wear at murder scenes on the TV news.

'It's your favourite colour!' he told her.

'Prussian blue?'

He beamed at her. 'How did you guess? Have you peeped?'

She simply pointed at him. 'It's splashed all over you!' she said with a scowl.

'I'm putting up new blinds too,' he told her.

'They'll probably fall down,' she replied. 'Everything you put up usually falls down after a short while.' *Just like your tiny weeny dick*, she nearly added.

Victor did not react to her rudeness. It no longer mattered. After a few nights sleeping in the spare room with the windows shut, she wouldn't be saying anything rude to him ever again.

They would find the cyanide in her at the post-mortem, of course. But the makers of the paint would be blamed. They would be in trouble for making a rogue batch of Prussian blue with too much cyanide in it. He just had to make sure no one ever found the tins he used, but getting rid of them would be easy.

On Sunday night, when he had finished, he left the spare-bedroom window wide open. He told Joan it was to let the paint dry. She would be able to start using the room from Monday night onwards, whenever he snored. And blimey, was he planning to snore tomorrow night! He would snore like he'd never snored before. He would snore for England!

Joan watched Victor drive off to work the next day in his usual cheery Monday morning mood. He was even more cheery than usual, she thought, despite the fact that this was the start of his last week at work.

She had too much on her mind to dwell on this. She busied herself with the household chores. Later it would be time to catch the bus for her afternoon shift at the supermarket. She needed to put on a good show of normality, so she gathered all Victor's dirty underwear from the laundry basket to do a wash. She was a little surprised that his boiler suit was not in there. She hunted everywhere, wondering where he might have left it, but she could not find it.

Never mind, she thought, with a wicked smile. With her plan, he wouldn't need it again. Not where he was going . . .

Chapter Seven

Every human being has a weak spot. Victor's was his diabetes, Joan knew. Too much sugar and he would fall sound asleep. Then he would snore like an elephant, keeping her awake all night. Her plan was simple. All she needed to do was to swap the insulin in his needle for sugar and he would go into a deep sleep. A very deep sleep.

While he was asleep she would inject some more sugar. Then some more still.

Until he stopped snoring. Until he stopped breathing.

She had it planned, to sweet perfection.

On this Monday evening of his last week at work, Victor arrived home and opened the front door with his latch key. He was surprised by what he found. His wife was stark naked, except for a black lace bra and a matching thong, and she was standing in red high-heeled shoes. She reeked of perfume.

'Aren't you cold?' he said. It was mid-February.

'I thought you might like a blow job, my darling husband!' she said.

'Actually, not really,' he replied. He did not add that he'd just had one at the Kitten Parlour. 'I think I'd prefer a beer. You look cold. You've got goose pimples.'

'I can warm you up, my darling,' she replied.

'I'm warm,' he said. 'But I'm worried about you.'

She brushed up sexily against him, and pressed her fingers against his crotch. 'Let's go to bed, my angel,' she said.

'Thanks, but *Poirot*'s on at nine o'clock.'

'We can record it.'

'I'd rather watch it now.'

She kissed him. 'Tell me, my angel, if you were to be hanged in the morning, what would your last meal be?'

He thought for a moment, then answered,

'Prawn cocktail, rib-eye steak, mushrooms, tomatoes, chips and peas. Followed by hot chocolate pudding with hot chocolate sauce. Why?'

'Well, that's a coincidence!' she said. 'Guess what's for supper?'

'Don't tell me you have all that?'

'For my darling Victor, nothing less would be good enough!'

Joan thought that the hot chocolate pudding with hot chocolate sauce would mask the amount of sugar.

Victor wondered if she had been drinking. Maybe she had been taking drugs. Or perhaps she wanted a car of her own instead of having to share his?

In your dreams! he thought.

Soon after finishing the meal he fell asleep on the sofa, with Poirot busily solving a crime in front of him.

She texted Don, as planned.

Twenty minutes later, Don arrived at the Smileys' front door. But the frown on his face was not part of their plan.

'There's a problem,' he said.

Chapter Eight

'I've just been watching *CSI*,' Don said, removing Joan's arms from around his neck.

'I like *CSI*,' she said. She liked it because Victor did not. It was too modern for his taste.

'Yep, well, you wouldn't have liked this one tonight. It was about diabetics. Right?'

Something about the way he said it made her shiver. 'Tell me.'

'Several diabetics have been murdered by people giving them overdoses. In some cases they give too much insulin, in others they give too much sugar. They have new forensic ways of testing. We can't risk it! We're going to have to get rid of the body.'

'No!' she said. 'That's not the plan! We agreed I would call the doctor in the morning, after he's nice and cold. That's the plan.'

'It doesn't work any more,' Don replied. 'They'll know he's had a massive sugar overdose.'

'I could tell them he's been depressed since losing his job. I could forge a suicide note,' she added helpfully.

'Too dangerous.'

'No one will know!' Joan replied. 'How will they know?'

'Handwriting experts!' Don hissed. He looked down at Victor and was startled to see his eyes struggling to open. Hastily, he stepped back, out of sight.

'But where would we put the body?' she said.

'Did you say something about a blow job?' Victor slurred.

'A blow job, my darling husband? Coming up!' Joan said. 'Just wait two minutes for the blow job of your life, my darling!'

She hurried into the kitchen and pulled on her yellow rubber gloves. Then she dashed into the garage where Victor's tools were hanging neatly from their hooks. She selected a medium-weight claw hammer and hurried back into the lounge. Holding the hammer behind her back, she said, 'Would you like your blow job now, my darling?'

Victor nodded. 'Yerrrr.'

Before Don even noticed what she was holding, Joan brought the hammer down hard on the side of Victor's forehead. She had never hit anyone on the side of the forehead with a claw hammer before, so she did not know quite what to expect.

Looking at him as soon as she had hit him, she thought that she would not need to hit quite so hard another time. Her stomach heaved and shockwaves pulsed through her. She took one more look at him, then ran into the kitchen and threw up in the sink.

She went back and peered at him. Neither man had moved. Don stood still, his eyes wide open, his mouth open even more.

'Bloody hell,' he gasped.

Victor lay still, with his skull cracked open like a broken coconut, blood spurting in all directions. His eyeballs bulged, unseeing, from their sockets. His tongue had shot out and stayed out. An orange and grey goo of brains leaked through his shattered temple.

Don said, 'I think he's brown bread.'

Joan had heard cockney rhyming slang in gangster films. She knew what brown bread meant. It meant *dead*.

She said nothing.

There was hair and blood on the end of the hammer. She stared at it, as if she had just performed some conjuring trick. *Now I have a clean hammer. Abracadabra! Now I have blood and hair on it!*

Now she had a dead husband.

A dead husband leaking blood and brains onto the sofa.

Leaking forensic evidence.

She put the hammer down on the floor and started shaking wildly, as she began to realize just what she had done.

She looked at Don in desperation. He was staring at Victor, wide-eyed, his mouth still open, shaking his head from side to side. 'Oh God,' he said. 'Oh Jesus.' Then he looked back at her.

She had no idea what was going through his mind.

'Why – why did you have to hit him so hard?' he asked.

42

'You'd have hit him softer, would you?'

After some moments, Don said, 'This is probably not the time for an argument.'

Chapter Nine

In the utility room off the kitchen, Joan had a big chest freezer squeezed in next to the washing machine and the tumble dryer. Victor had got angry when she'd bought the freezer. He told her it was a waste of money and where the hell were they going to put it?

Joan had replied that it would pay for itself because of all the sell-by-date bargains she could buy in her supermarket. Now she stood over it, with the lid open and icy vapour rising. She was pulling out all those bargains she had been piling into it for the past year.

Out came a packet of lamb cutlets with a *Special Offer!* sticker. Then came a big bag of frozen peas and a huge tub of Wall's vanilla ice cream. There were three chocolate cheesecakes that she had been planning to eat by herself.

She thought they were too good to share with Victor! She handed each item to Don, who placed them on the floor.

Every few moments she would peer out of the window. They had drawn the curtains and blinds on all the other windows downstairs, just in case anyone happened to peer in. However, the blind on this window had fallen down months ago. Lazy Victor had never bothered to put it back up again.

She could see the lights of the houses in the valley below and the dark outline of the Downs in the distance. She could see the stars and the rising moon. It was almost a full moon. In the light from it she could see the little greenhouse in the garden. She thought for a moment about the tomatoes Victor had planted. He was never going to see them, or eat them. Victor wasn't even going to see daylight ever again.

For a moment, just for a tiny moment, she had a choking feeling in her throat. Victor wasn't so bad, she thought to herself. Not really so bad, was he? He had good points, didn't he?

Don's voice cut harshly through her thoughts. 'Come on, keep it coming, nearly done!'

She stooped over, reached down to the bottom and pulled up a frozen sponge cake in its box. Then some *Special Reduction* pork chops.

'Okay,' she said. 'That's it.'

Then she peered in, nervously, all her thoughts in turmoil. What if he did not fit?

Five minutes later, Don and Joan had removed all Victor's clothes. They also took off his watch and his wedding band.

'No point letting anything go to waste,' Joan had said.

Then they struggled to carry his fat, blubbery body through the kitchen and into the tiny utility room. They left a trail of blood spots and brain-fluid droplets as they went.

It was lucky Don was strong because Joan felt she had no strength left in her. With some pushing and shoving, they got Victor up over the lip of the freezer. Then, to her relief, he slid down easily to the bottom. She just needed to arrange his arms and legs so they would not obstruct the lid. All the time, Joan avoided looking at his bulging eyes. In fact, she avoided looking at any part of him.

She couldn't help glimpsing his tiny penis, though. *That's the bit of you I'll be missing least of all*, she thought. Then she began to pile the frozen foods back in on top of him.

'Hope he doesn't wake up feeling hungry,' Don said, as he finally slammed the lid down.

Joan looked at him in shock. 'You don't think—?'

He laid his big, meaty hand on her shoulder and gave her a squeeze. 'He's dead, don't worry. He's as dead as dead gets.'

They spent the rest of the evening cleaning. They scrubbed the downstairs carpets and the kitchen floor. They had to scrub the living-room walls too, because they found spots of blood and brain fluid there as well. There were more on the ceiling and on one of the lamp-shades. A spot of blood was even on the television screen.

'Hope Poirot doesn't notice this one,' Don said, wiping the tiny fleck from the screen.

Joan did not smile.

Chapter Ten

Shortly before midnight, exhausted from cleaning, and shaking from too much coffee, Don had to go home. He would be back first thing in the morning, he said.

Joan stayed downstairs for a long time. She stared at the dents in the armchair cushions where Victor had been sitting when she'd hit him. The house was silent. The air felt heavy, as if it was pushing down on her. She could hear the occasional tick of the fridge. But she didn't dare go into the kitchen on her own, not tonight, not while it was dark.

Eventually, she went upstairs. The bathroom smelled of Victor's colognes and aftershaves. The bedroom smelled of him too, but not so strongly. There were a couple of strands of his hair in the basin. That was another thing that annoyed her about him. He was always leaving hairs in the basin, the lazy bugger. He could never be bothered to remove them. She scooped them up now with a tissue. It was the last time she would have to do that, she thought with some small joy, as she dropped them into the pedal bin. The lid shut with a loud clang that startled her.

God, I'm jumpy, she thought. Hardly surprising.

She drew the bathroom curtain, then went through into the bedroom and closed the curtains there. She hoped none of the nosy neighbours were looking out of their windows. They would think it odd that it was after two in the morning and she was closing the bedroom curtains. She and Victor were normally in bed by eleven.

She took off all her clothes and put them in a black bin liner, as Don had instructed. He was going to take them to the municipal tip in the morning. He would also take Victor's clothes and the hammer, which he had put into the bottom tray of his toolbox.

After pulling on her nightdress, she swallowed two aspirins. She removed Victor's striped pyjamas from his side of the bed and put them on the floor. Then she climbed into the empty bed, which smelled of Victor, and switched the light off. She switched it back on again at once. The darkness scared her tonight. So much was buzzing in her head. There was a list of things she had to do tomorrow, which she had worked out with Don.

She stared at the blank television screen on the shelf just beyond the end of the bed. She looked at Victor's brown leather slippers on the floor and at the Agatha Christie novel on his bedside table. She listened to the silence of the night. It seemed so loud. She heard a faint, tinny ringing in her ears. The distant wail of a siren from a police car, or an ambulance, or perhaps a fire engine. Then the screech of two cats fighting. One of them was probably Gregory, she thought. She watched her bedside clock.

2.59 a.m.

Then 3.00 a.m.

Then 3.01 a.m.

She turned on the television. There was a

medium she recognized, talking to a studio audience. 'I have someone with me called Mary,' he said. 'Is there anyone here who has recently lost someone called Mary?'

Normally, she liked these shows. But tonight it made her uneasy.

She switched channels. *Big Brother.* Two young men and a fat blonde girl were sitting in a giant ashtray, smoking. She listened to their chatter for some minutes, then switched channels again. An old movie was playing. Glenn Close was in her house. Suddenly, a black, gloved fist smashed a window and opened the door from the inside.

She hastily switched channels once more. Then looked at the clock again.

3.14

She needed to pee. All that damned coffee! She got out of bed, padded out of the room and into the bathroom. She peed, then went to the basin to rinse her hands.

And froze.

Two long, black strands of Victor's hair were lying there.

Chapter Eleven

'You imagined it!' Don said when he came round at nine o'clock in the morning.

'No, Don, I did not,' Joan said. Her hands were shaking so much she could hardly open the tin of cat food. 'I did not imagine it!'

'Of course you did. Your nerves are all shot to hell!'

Her eyes felt raw from lack of sleep. There was a tight band across her scalp. 'I did not imagine it! I looked in the pedal bin and the hairs I took out were still there, in the tissue.'

She scraped the stinky cat food out of the can into Gregory's bowl and put it on the floor. As usual, the cat glared at the bowl, and then at her, as if suspecting poison.

'You must have missed them, love,' Don

said. 'We were both tired!' He put his arms around her and hugged her tightly. Then he nuzzled her ear. 'Let's go to bed, I'm feeling really horny.'

She pushed him away. 'I did *not miss* those hairs. And we can't go to bed. I have to go to the police, like you told me. And I have to go to work. You said we have to act normal.'

'Yeah, *normal*! So let's go to bed. That would be *normal*.'

'Not with Victor in the freezer, no way!'

'Come on, angel. We did this so we could be together.'

She looked at him. 'I can't. It wouldn't be right. I don't feel in the mood. Okay?'

They stared at each other in silence.

'It's all right for you, Don. You went home to your little wifey. I had to stay here alone with my husband in the bloody freezer.'

'Yeah, right, so?'

'So?' she repeated, her anger rising. '*So?* Is that all you can bloody say?'

'I love you,' he said.

'I love you too. We – we just have to—'

'To what?'

She shook her head. Tears rolled down her cheeks. 'You have to help me, Don.'

'We have to stay calm.'

'I AM BLOODY CALM!' she yelled.

He raised his big hands and stood there in front of her. A big tall guy, in his brown leather jacket over a white T-shirt, jeans and suede boots, he was all manly. 'Okay,' he said. 'Okay!'

'It's not okay!'

'So, we have to make it okay. Right?' He held her in his arms again.

'Right,' she whispered. 'The plan. We have to stick to the plan.'

'We'll stick to the plan,' he said. 'So you mustn't get freaked out by two hairs you missed in your basin. Deal?'

'Deal,' she agreed glumly.

Half an hour later, Joan drove to Brighton Police Station. Victor's purple Vauxhall Astra convertible had been an eBay bargain three years ago. She parked at a meter and went in through the front door. There was a second door marked *IN*, with a short queue on the far side of it.

She joined the queue, and as she waited she read some of the notices on the walls. One was headed *MISSING PERSONS*. There were several photographs, close-ups of faces, with the same wording at the bottom of each one:

IF YOU HAVE SEEN THIS PERSON PLEASE CONTACT YOUR NEAREST POLICE STATION.

Joan didn't recognize any of them. She read another notice, warning about alcohol abuse, and another about drugs. Finally, she reached the front desk. A woman in her thirties, wearing a white shirt and a black tie, asked if she could help her.

Joan was glad the woman could not see her knees. They were trembling. 'I want to report a missing person,' she said.

'All right,' the woman said. 'Can you give me some details?'

'Victor ... my husband. He didn't come home last night. I'm worried because ... he ... this ... he ... this is very unusual ... I mean ... not unusual ... I mean ... he has never in his life not come home ... in the evening ... after work.' Joan felt her face burning. She was stumbling over the words. She felt hot and confused. 'He doesn't ... you know ... I mean ... he always does ... come home ... my husband.'

There was a brief silence. Suddenly, in this silence, all Joan could think about were the two hairs in the washbasin.

'I see,' the woman said. 'And you are?' She picked up a pen.

'His wife,' Joan said, dumbly, her voice trembling. She could feel sweat trickling down her neck.

'Your name?' the woman said patiently.

'Yes, yes. I'm Joan. Mrs ... er ... Mrs Smiley.'

The woman wrote this down. 'If you could step aside and wait for a moment, I'll get an officer to come and take down some details.'

Joan stepped aside. The woman went over to the phone. One of her colleagues attended to the next person in the queue behind Joan. A young girl, who looked spaced out, reported she had lost her mobile phone.

Joan took some deep breaths, trying to calm

down. She watched several more people in turn step up to the counter. But she wasn't listening to them. She was trying to rehearse what Don had told her to say.

'Mrs Smiley?'

Joan turned at the sound of her name, and saw a tubby young woman with short fair hair. She was wearing a black uniform waistcoat over a white shirt and black trousers. The officer was peering at the people in the room.

Joan raised a hand. 'Yes, that's me.'

The officer had a radio sticking out of her breast pocket. A badge on one side of her chest bore a police crest with the words *BRIGHTON AND HOVE*. A badge on the other side said *COMMUNITY SUPPORT*. 'Would you come this way, please?' she said.

Joan followed her through the door, along a corridor and into a cramped, windowless room. There was only a metal table with chairs either side of it. 'I'm PCSO Watts,' she said politely, but very seriously.

'Nice to meet you,' Joan replied. She was now drenched in sweat.

The Police Community Support Officer

asked her to sit down. Then PCSO Watts sat on the other side of the table. She opened a large notebook with a printed form on it. 'Your husband is missing, is that right, Mrs Smiley?'

Joan nodded.

PCSO Watts picked up a biro. 'Right, let's start with his name.'

'Victor Joseph Smiley,' she said.

The officer wrote this down, very slowly. 'And his age?'

'Forty-three.'

'You are worried because he did not come home last night, is that correct?'

Joan nodded. She did not like the way the officer was looking at her, studying her face intently. It felt as if she was looking right through her. 'It's very unusual,' Joan said. 'I mean, more than unusual, if you see what I mean?'

The officer frowned. 'I'm afraid I don't, no.'

'Victor's never done this before. Not come home. Not ever in all the time we've been married.'

'Which is how long?'

'Nineteen and a half years,' Joan replied. She could have added, *three weeks, four days, sixteen hours and seven minutes too long.*

For the next quarter of an hour Joan felt she was on trial. The officer fired one question after another at her. Had Joan contacted any of their friends? Yes, Ted and Madge, but they had not seen him or heard from him. What about Victor's relatives? All he had was a sister, in Melbourne.

The officer wrote each answer down, painfully slowly.

Joan did her best to talk about Victor in a way she thought any loving wife would talk about her husband. He was the perfect man in every way. She adored him. He adored her. They had never spent a single day apart in all the years they had been married. Of course, they had their ups and downs, like any couple. She said that he was feeling very low after being made redundant. Very, very low.

But he had never, ever, not come home. Until last night.

Even after Joan said all this, PCSO Watts

asked if this had ever happened before. Joan told her again that it had not. She repeated that he had been feeling low after being told he was being made redundant.

PCSO Watts was kind and full of sympathy. 'Have you tried phoning his mobile number?' she asked.

Joan went white for an instant. She felt her stomach churn like a cement mixer. The officer went in and out of focus. *That stupid fool, Don! Why the hell didn't he tell me to do that? How could I have been so stupid not to have thought of it?*

'Oh yes,' she said. 'I try all the time. I keep phoning and phoning him.'

'Are you worried about the effect that losing his job might have had on him and on his pride?' PCSO Watts asked.

'He is a proud man,' Joan said. Well, she thought, that was better than saying *he was an arrogant tosser.*

'Do you have a photograph of him we could circulate?' Juliet Watts asked.

'I could find one,' she said.

'That would be very helpful.'

'I'll drop one in.'

'Look,' the officer said, 'I know this might be difficult for you, but is it possible that Victor is having an affair?'

Joan shook her head. 'No. He loves me. We are very close. We are very, very close.'

'So, you are worried about his state of mind after losing his job?'

'I am very worried,' Joan said. Don had told her to focus on this. Don had told her to try to make the police think he might have killed himself. 'Victor is such a proud man. He came home in tears and sobbed his heart out the day he heard the news.'

That was a big fib, of course. He'd come home blind drunk, telling her he'd just told his boss where to stick his job!

'Are you worried that he might have killed himself, Mrs Smiley?'

'Yes.'

As she drove away from the police station, Joan was pleased with herself. She thought she had come across rather well as the desperate, sad wife of a missing person.

PCSO Juliet Watts had a different opinion. 'Not happy about this person,' she wrote in her report.

Chapter Twelve

Yes, Joan thought, she did feel pleased with herself. She decided she had handled herself well. She had given a great performance. PCSO Watts had believed her. That was important. It was also important that the officer said she was marking Victor down as *High Risk*.

Success!

She could not wait to tell Don.

She had to act normally first, so she did her afternoon shift, as usual, at the supermarket. But her mind was not on it and she kept making mistakes. Then at six o'clock, on the dot, she left and drove home. Not having to wait for the bus was a luxury in itself.

When she turned into her road, the sight of a white van in her driveway sent a bolt of fear through her. The van was backed right up against the garage door.

Joan parked in the street, hurried to the door and let herself in. Don was standing in the hall, in grimy jeans and a filthy T-shirt. Sweat was pouring off him. He was so covered in grey dust he looked like a ghost. 'How did it go?' he asked.

'What's the van? Whose is it?' she blurted anxiously.

'Calm down, love. Don't I get a kiss?'

Ignoring him, she repeated anxiously, 'Whose van is it?' As she asked she was looking at the hall table, to see if Victor's mobile phone was there.

'Relax! I borrowed the van from a mate. I'll show you what I used it for in a moment. So?'

'So?'

'So, how did it go at the cop shop?'

'It was a breeze!'

'See, you're a star!' He hugged her and tried to kiss her on the lips, but she turned her face, so he kissed her cheek instead. Then she pulled away from him.

'You're all sweaty,' she said.

'I've been working, while you've been acting the star!'

She did not feel like a star. She felt in need of a drink. She wanted a glass of wine. After that, she thought she would want another, and another.

Then she would probably want one more.

'I need to phone Victor,' she said.

'You'd get a shock if he answered!'

'That's not funny. The police officer asked if I'd phoned him. We should have thought of the phone. That was stupid. Why didn't you think of it?'

He shrugged and shook his head. 'Dunno. Slipped my mind.'

'Great,' she said bitterly. 'What else didn't we think of? You had it all under control, you told me. You had it all planned. The perfect murder!'

'I did,' he nodded. 'That was before we knew about the sugar, and before you hit him.'

'You should have found out about the sugar sooner,' she said.

'Yeah, well, now we have to deal with things as they are. Don't worry, I have it all worked out.'

She took her mobile phone from her bag and

dialled Victor's number. His Nokia, on the hall table, rang six times then stopped. She listened, and moments later she heard his voice message.

'Hello, this is Victor Smiley. I'm sorry I can't take your call at the moment. I'm not available. Please leave me a message and I'll call you back.'

It was strange hearing his voice. It made her feel all tingly, in a bad way. Feeling very self-conscious, Joan said, 'Hello, Victor dear. Where are you? Please call me. I am so worried about you, and I'm missing you. Love you!'

'Liar!' Don said when she hung up. 'You don't love him!'

Her face was burning, as if it was on fire. 'You can't lie to a dead person, can you?'

'We need to hide his phone,' Don said. 'Remind me to take it later and ditch it somewhere. You shouldn't have left that message. That was stupid. That was really stupid.'

'It would have been even more stupid not to.'

'It was stupid,' he repeated. 'You're panicking. We mustn't panic.'

'I need a drink,' she said.

Don insisted they went to the garage first. They had work to do, he said.

She followed him through the door that led from the hall to the garage. It was draughty in there and the concrete floor was cold under her feet. The air was so thick with dust she could barely see. It prickled her throat and she coughed.

Normally, they parked the Astra in here at night, but there would be no room now. In the centre of the garage there was a hole that Don had been digging. It was about six feet long and three feet wide. Concrete rubble and earth were scattered either side of it. Stacked against the far wall were several sacks of ready-mixed concrete, a pick-axe, two garden spades and several more tools.

'There we are,' Don said proudly. 'I've been busy today. I'm a one-man VDT.'

'VDT?' she said. 'What's that?'

'Victor Disposal Team!'

'That's not funny,' she said.

'Come on, love. You're the one who wanted

to do away with him. You asked me to help you. I'm helping you.'

She looked down into the grave. It was about two feet deep. 'It's too shallow,' she said.

'I'm not finished. We're going to put him down a good six feet. Don't want the smell to start getting out when he decomposes.'

Victor was the man she used to love and sleep with. Joan's stomach suddenly churned at the thought of him rotting. 'You're not – you're not serious? You're going to bury Victor *here*?'

'Too right.'

'In my garage?'

'It's perfect! I used to be a bricklayer, remember? I can do a perfect concrete screed. No one will ever know.'

'What about *me*?' she said. 'I will know.'

Then the front doorbell rang.

Both of them froze, looking at each other. 'Who's that?' Don said.

'I dunno.' Joan raised a finger to her lips for him to keep quiet. She went out into the hall, closing the internal garage door behind her. She coughed again from the dust. As she went near the front door, the bell rang again.

She hurried up the stairs and into the room that Victor used as his den. She peered down through the window.

Two police officers were standing outside her front door.

Chapter Thirteen

They were both male, wearing their black uniform waistcoats and police caps with chequered bands. She studied them for a moment and could see they were looking impatient. Then she hurried downstairs to tell Don to wait quietly in the garage. As she opened the front door, her nerves were jangling. 'Sorry to keep you waiting, I – I was on the loo.'

'Mrs Smiley?' said the older of the two men, holding up his warrant card. 'Sergeant Rose and PC Black from Brighton Police.'

'Yes,' she said, 'hello.' Then, quick as a flash, she added, 'Have you got any news about Victor? Have you found my husband?'

'No, I'm afraid not, madam. We presume you have not heard from him either?'

'No.'

'May we come in?'

'Yes, yes, of course. Thank you, thank you for coming.'

She moved so that they could come into the hall. Both men took their caps off. Sergeant Rose was in his forties. His hair was short and black, with some grey. He had a pleasant face and a brisk but friendly manner. His colleague was in his mid-twenties. He was tall and rather gangly, with short blond hair gelled into spikes.

As she led them through into the lounge, she noticed Victor's phone sitting on the hall table. For a moment she felt panic, then she realized they would not know it was his.

She pointed at the settee and the two policemen sat down on it, holding their caps on their laps. She sat opposite them in an armchair and did her best to look sad.

Sergeant Rose took out a notebook and the constable did the same. 'Is that your van in the driveway, Mrs Smiley?' the sergeant asked.

'The – the white one?' Joan said, as if there was a whole line of vans parked in the driveway, in a range of different colours.

The two police officers exchanged a brief glance, which made Joan even more uneasy.

'The white one, yes,' Sergeant Rose said.

'No – er – that's not mine – ours – er – that's the plumber's van.'

'Got a problem with your drains, have you?' the constable asked.

Joan felt herself breaking out in sweat. She remembered a TV show that Victor had watched, about the serial killer Dennis Nilsen. Nilsen murdered young men and chopped them up in his kitchen. Then he flushed parts of them down the sink and parts down the loo. He was caught when the drains became blocked and the plumbing firm found human remains in them.

Rising panic tightened her throat so much that her voice came out as a squeak. 'No. No, nothing like that! Just – er – new bathroom taps and a new shower. Victor and I are having a bathroom makeover.'

The sergeant nodded. There was silence for a few moments. Then the constable said, 'For a workman, your plumber's very quiet.'

'He is,' Joan said. 'Good as gold! You wouldn't know he was here.'

'Apart from the van outside,' Sergeant Rose said.

Joan nodded. 'Yes, well, of course, apart from that!'

There was another silence, longer and more awkward than the last one. Then Sergeant Rose said, 'We've come round, Mrs Smiley, because we have some concerns about your husband.'

'Thank you,' she said. 'I'm very grateful.' She took a handkerchief from her handbag and dabbed her eyes. 'I feel so terrible,' she said. 'So terrible.'

He glanced down at some writing in his notebook. 'On the Missing Persons Report you stated that your husband is diabetic. Do you know if he had his medication with him?'

'I – I would think so,' she said. 'He always had it with him.'

'Have you checked whether he took it with him yesterday? Sunday evening was the last time you saw him, correct?'

'Yes,' she said. 'Sunday evening, that was the last time.'

'Can you repeat the events of Sunday for me?'

She felt the heat burning her face. Her body felt slippery with sweat. She needed to make sure she said the same thing to these officers as she had said to the officer at the police station.

'I wasn't feeling well. Victor was home. I went to bed early and left him downstairs watching television. In the morning, he was gone. At first, I thought he'd left for work early, but it was strange because he always brought me a cup of tea before he went.'

'What was his state of mind after losing his job, Mrs Smiley?' the constable asked.

'Terrible. He was in shock. He'd given the best years of his life to those sods at that company. It destroyed him, being let go like that. He was a broken man. He just sat here weeping in this room, night after night.'

Joan paused, feeling a little more confident. She was calming down and getting into her stride. 'He told me several times in the past few weeks that he didn't want to go on living. He couldn't face not being wanted any more. He was broken, totally broken.'

The sergeant frowned. 'We went round to the premises of Stanley Smith & Son on the Hollingbury industrial estate this afternoon. That's where your husband is, or was, employed, isn't it?'

She nodded, not liking the sound of this.

'We talked to several of his colleagues, trying to find out the state of his mind. Everyone we spoke to said he seemed very happy.' He looked down at his notes again. 'One said that yesterday, the first day of his last week with the company, he was humming and smiling a lot. He was telling them he felt free for the first time in his life. He said that he was going to enjoy himself. He said that life was too short to spend all of it in an office.'

'That's my Victor,' she said, pressing her eyelids tightly together. She was trying to make herself cry or at least squeeze out a couple of tears. 'He was such a proud man.'

'*Was*?' said the constable, sharply.

'What *am* I saying! See what a state I'm in! Is. *Is*. My darling Victor *is* such a proud man. He wouldn't let those sods think they had won!' She dabbed her eyes with her handkerchief.

'Oh yes, he gave them all a good show, trying to let them think he didn't care. But inside, he was broken. He just came home and wept and wept and wept. Please find him for me. Please find him. I'm terrified he might have gone and done something rash. My poor darling. My Victor. I couldn't live without him.'

'We'll try our best,' they promised as they left.

At that moment, Victor's phone began to warble. Joan closed the door, went to the table and picked it up. It was ringing and vibrating in her hand. *Private Number* showed on the display. She daren't answer it, she realized. So she let it continue for several more rings until it stopped.

Then she checked to see if the caller had left a message. But they hadn't.

Chapter Fourteen

Downstairs, in the basement of the Kitten Parlour, was a rest room. It had comfy chairs and a television so that the girls could relax while they were waiting for clients.

At seven o'clock in the evening, Kamila put down her mobile phone. She lit a cigarette, then took a sip of her coffee. She was worried about Victor. He hadn't called or texted last night at all, nor all day today.

He was constantly phoning, and leaving her text messages. He would usually send her two or three texts during the night, and he always called her from his office in the morning. This was not like him. Kamila badly needed to speak to him. Kaspar, her boyfriend, had found out she was in Brighton and he knew where she was living. He left threatening messages on her voicemail. Victor had promised to take care of her.

She liked Victor. He was funny. He made her feel safe. The most important thing was that he was a very rich man! He would be able to get rid of Kaspar. He'd promised her that. He had contacts in high places. Kaspar would be history.

Now he had vanished and she desperately hoped that it was not Victor who was history. She did not dare to leave a message, because Victor had told her never to do that.

Nervously, she smoked her cigarette down to the butt. She was about to light another when the maid upstairs called her name on the intercom.

'Kamila, you have a client!'

She hurried up the stairs, hopeful that it might be Victor. It wasn't, of course.

Chapter Fifteen

After the police left, Don drove off in the van. He couldn't leave it in the driveway all evening or the neighbours would wonder about it, he said. He parked it a couple of streets away, then walked back. He was dressed in black and was barely visible in the darkness.

At eleven o'clock, Joan came into the garage with about the tenth mug of coffee for him. By then, his head could hardly be seen. Earth was piled high on either side of the grave, and scattered across the garage floor. The smell of dust was less strong now. Instead, there was a musty smell of damp soil.

Joan was cold and exhausted and covered in dirt. Her hands were blistered from when she had taken over the digging a couple of times, while Don had a rest.

She was still not at all happy about burying Victor here, in their garage.

'It's the best place,' Don said. 'Trust me! If you look at how most murderers get caught, it's because a body turns up somewhere. A body is found in a shallow grave in the woods, or washed up on a beach. Or they get caught trying to get rid of the body. If there is no body, then there is nothing for the police to go on. They've no reason to suspect you anyway, have they?'

'No,' Joan agreed. She did feel that the police were just a little bit suspicious. But what Don said did make sense.

So she stood and watched as he dug deeper and deeper. Slowly but steadily he was getting there, bit by bit by bit.

A few minutes past midnight, Joan helped Don heave her husband's body out of the freezer. Victor was hard and cold and his flesh was a grey colour, with specks of frost on it. She avoided looking at his face. She didn't want to catch his eye.

They half carried, half dragged him into the

hall, and then into the garage. Then they hauled him over the mounds of freshly dug earth and into the long, narrow hole.

For one horrible moment, Joan thought the hole was *too* narrow. Victor's body fell a couple of feet, but his shoulders and stomach got wedged.

Don sat down on the side and gave him a shove with his feet. Victor slithered and tumbled like a huge Guy Fawkes dummy. He landed with a hard thud in the wet earth at the bottom.

'Have some respect,' Joan said. 'You shouldn't have pushed him with your feet.'

'Pardon me,' Don said. 'Why don't you phone the sodding vicar and ask him to come round here? He could hold a proper burial service.'

Joan said nothing. She stared down at the naked, ungainly heap that had once been the man she loved. She felt a whole raft of emotions. She felt sadness, fear, guilt.

She felt no joy.

She had thought that she would feel joy from the moment he was dead. She had expected her love for Don would be so much stronger. But she did not feel any love for him at all right now. In fact, she wished he would go away and leave her alone. She wanted to say a private goodbye to Victor.

She knelt, scooped up a handful of earth and dropped it on the corpse. Then she whispered, so quietly that Don could not hear, 'Goodbye, my love. It wasn't all bad, was it?'

Then she stood up and helped Don to shovel the earth back in.

It was after one o'clock by the time they had finished. Joan was almost asleep on her feet. 'Isn't your wife going to be wondering where you are?' she asked.

He glanced at his watch. 'Mandy'll be asleep. I told her I was working late. I have to do an early morning pick-up from Heathrow airport, so I warned her I might work through the night.' He gave her a peck on the cheek. 'Don't worry.'

Joan swept all the loose soil onto the mound of the grave, while Don walked up and down, to flatten it. Finally, it was level with the garage floor.

They had another coffee. Don cut open the first bag of ready-mixed cement. Joan went to fetch a bucket of water from the kitchen. Then, steadily, Don began to cover the entire floor with cement. Bit by bit by bit.

By four o'clock in the morning, the job was done. All his tools and the empty sacks of cement were in the hall. He would bring the van round later to collect them. 'What do you think?' he said, putting his arm around her.

She peered in through the door at the glistening, wet cement. It was impossible to see where the grave had been dug. The floor was perfect, flat and even.

'Yes,' she said. 'It's good.'

'Mustn't walk on it until tomorrow.'

'No.'

'I don't think Victor's going anywhere!' he said.

They stared at each other and then Don gave her a hug. 'It'll all be fine,' he said. 'Just stay calm and no one will be any the wiser. Tomorrow afternoon, after you finish work, we'll have a drink. Yeah? In bed, yeah?'

Joan bit her lip. With Victor under the

garage floor, she did not know how she felt. She nodded, and gave him a thin smile.

He opened the front door and slipped out into the night. Joan closed the door and pressed down the latch lock. Then, feeling a strange sense that she was being watched, she turned round.

Victor was standing halfway up the stairs, looking at her.

Chapter Sixteen

She screamed, but only silent air came out of her throat. She screamed again, but still her voice would not work. Her whole body was shaking. She closed her eyes and backed up against the door. She fumbled with her hands behind her back to open it. Then she opened her eyes.

Victor had gone.

Upstairs? Had he gone upstairs?

Her heart was crashing around inside her chest. She was gulping down air. She looked up at the dark landing and listened.

Listened.

Silence.

There was a loud clatter in the kitchen, which nearly made her jump out of her skin. Then she realized it was just the cat flap.

Gregory slunk into the hall. He glared at her, as if he wanted to know what she was doing up so late, and in his space.

'Victor!' she called out. Her voice was suddenly working again, but it was very shrill. 'Victor?'

Silence.

Of course there was silence. She'd just buried him. It was just her imagination working overtime. Wasn't it?

Joan went through into the kitchen, deciding she was far too wide awake to sleep. Anyway, she did not dare to go up the stairs at the moment. She needed a drink, badly.

She took a bottle of wine out of the fridge and poured herself a glass. She drank it straight down and poured another. She was about to start drinking the second glass when the cat pawed at her leg.

'What is it?' she said, talking in a whisper, although there was no need. 'Hungry?'

The cat just looked at her. She had never liked the way Gregory looked at her, and she liked it even less now. It was as if he knew what she had just done. She opened a tin of food, scooped some of it into a bowl and placed it on the floor.

Straight away, Gregory turned and began staring at her again. Joan drained her glass, then poured a third. Within a few minutes, as the alcohol began to kick in, she started to feel a tiny bit better.

She had imagined Victor. That was all it was. Her mind was playing tricks because she was tired. She had been through a lot in the past twenty-four hours.

Suddenly, she smelled cigar smoke. The familiar smell of Victor's cigars. It was getting stronger by the second. Then there was a strange, ghastly hissing sound. It sent a bolt of fear through her, like electricity.

It was coming from Gregory. He was standing with his back arched and his fur raised on end. He was baring his teeth and hissing at the open door to her left.

A large, blue ring of cigar smoke was drifting in from the hall.

Chapter Seventeen

Joan ran out of the house, down her front garden and into the street. As she did so, the front door slammed behind her.

She stood, panting, in the faint yellow glow of the street light. Her heart was hammering and she was gulping air. Then she heard a vehicle. For a moment she was tempted to run into the middle of the road. She could shout for help and flag it down.

It was a police patrol car.

She stepped back, hastily, into the shadow of a bush. She was aware that she was filthy from head to toe, and that questions would be asked. She knew the police might want to know what she was doing up at this hour. Why had she run out of her house?

Christ, she thought. She stared up at the

house. She looked at the windows. It was as if she was expecting to see Victor peering out at her.

Victor didn't believe in ghosts. She liked to watch shows about mediums, but he always pooh-poohed them. He used to say, 'Tricks of the mind, that's all ghosts are. They're tricks of the mind.'

Had it been a trick of the mind when she saw Victor standing on the stairs? What about the ring of cigar smoke? What about his hairs in the basin yesterday?

The tail lights of the police car vanished around the corner. She shivered. An icy wind was blowing. A spot of rain struck her cheek. She was locked out, she realized. Locked out of her house by a ghost!

Bugger. Damn. Blast.

Her phone was inside. Everything was inside. She did not want to go back in, but where else could she go, especially at this hour? She could go round to Ted and Madge, but they lived about three miles away.

Then she remembered the spare key! Victor kept one under a brick by the back door. At least he used to. She just hoped it was still there.

She squeezed past the dustbins, opened the side gate and reached the step to the kitchen door. In the darkness, she found the brick, lifted it and felt the ground. To her relief the key was there. She scooped it safely into her palm. Then she went back around to the front of the house, unlocked the door and went in. She locked the door behind her, saying loudly, 'Tricks of the mind. That's all. Tricks of the mind!'

She was too afraid to go upstairs, so she rushed into the kitchen and shut herself in. The cat had run off somewhere, back into the night. The night was where he belonged, she thought.

Then she switched on the television for company and sat down at the table. Over the next twenty minutes she finished the entire bottle of wine.

Chapter Eighteen

Kamila had only gone to bed at 4 a.m. At 8.30 a.m. she was woken in her bedsit by the ringtone of her mobile phone.

She opened one eye and stared through her fringe of hair at the phone. She hoped it was Victor. Or was it Kaspar? *Please don't let it be Kaspar*, she thought. *It's too early. I can't put up with his anger so early.*

No numbers showed on the display. It simply said: Call.

She answered nervously. Was it Victor calling from a new phone? Was it Kaspar hiding his number?

A male voice she did not recognize said, 'Hello, this is Constable Black from Brighton and Hove Police.'

Kamila felt a stab of panic. Was she in

trouble for working at the Kitten Parlour? 'Yes?' she said anxiously.

'We are looking for Mr Victor Smiley, who has been missing since Monday evening. Calls to his mobile phone are being monitored, and it was reported to us that a call was made to his phone from your number at 6.55 p.m. yesterday. Are you the person who made the call?'

'Victor is missing?' she said.

'Yes. We are concerned for his safety. Are you a friend of his?'

'Yes,' she said in her broken English. 'I very good friend.'

Victor was missing? She closed her eyes for a moment, feeling gutted. What did this mean? Had something happened to him?

'We'd like to talk to you,' the constable said. 'Can we come over to see you? If you'd prefer, you could drop into Brighton Police Station.'

Kamila walked past the police station every day on her way to work. She always walked, to save the bus fare. She had to be at work by midday for the lunchtime trade. 'I can come about half past ten. Is okay?'

'That will be fine. May I have your name?'

She told him.

'At the front desk, ask for me, Constable Black.'

'Please, can you tell me, is Victor – is he okay?'

'We don't know. We are anxious to find him. We are concerned for his safety.'

Kamila thanked him, ended the call, and stood up. She was far too wide awake to sleep any more.

Concerned for his safety.

Victor was the only man who had ever been kind to her. The only person who offered her an escape from the horrible life she was stuck in. Now the police were concerned for his safety.

She would do everything she possibly could to help them. She stared at the phone again. *Please call. Victor. Please call!*

Then a thought struck her. Victor often talked to her about his wife. He said she was a bad person. That she made him very unhappy. She wondered if she should tell the police this.

Chapter Nineteen

'You look like shit,' Don said.

'Well, thank you, lover boy! You certainly know how to make a girl feel great!'

Joan sat at the kitchen table with a blinding hangover and no make-up. She'd had about one hour's sleep. She *felt* like shit.

There were three messages on her mobile phone. They were all from Madge, who had rung last night. Joan had been busy in the garage with Don and had not heard her phone ring. Madge said that she and Ted had had a visit from the police, who told them that Victor was still missing. Was she okay? Why hadn't she called them? Would she like them to pop round?

'Don, Victor was here in the house last night. It was after you left,' she said.

'Then he should change his name to Houdini!' Don said. 'If he's capable of getting out from under six feet of earth and a concrete screed!'

'Victor *was* here,' she said.

'Was the Pope here too?' he asked.

'I'm serious.'

Don stroked her hair. 'It's going to be tough, love, but we have to keep calm. Yeah? Keep cool, right?'

'Easy for you to say. You weren't here.'

'Ghosts don't exist,' he said.

Joan stared at him, angry that he doubted her. She looked at him, sitting across the table. She realized he wasn't the big, powerful hero that he had seemed only a few days ago. In his leather jacket, sweatshirt and jeans, with his close-cropped hair and his weathered face, he looked weak. He looked so bloody weak. Victor, despite all his faults, suddenly seemed twice the man that Don was.

He got up and tried to kiss her, but she jerked back.

'Come on, love, what's the matter?'

She said nothing. She turned her face away

from his and stared out at the garden. She looked at the lawn Victor had tended and at Victor's shed. She looked at the greenhouse, with Victor's tomato plants. She looked at the flower beds, at the plants that Victor had dead-headed. 'Just take the stuff you were coming to collect. Take it and get rid of it!'

'I love you,' he said.

She turned and stared past Don. She gazed at the open doorway where she had seen the ring of tobacco smoke drift in, just a few hours earlier. *Shit*, she thought. *Shit, shit, shit, what have I done?*

Then her phone rang. It was Madge's number on the display. Joan answered.

'Joan! Joan, love! Is this true? Has Victor left you? I tried to get hold of you all night! How are you?'

Joan swallowed. Then she began to sob down the phone.

'Joan, I'm coming over! What you need is some company!'

'No, no, I'm fine.'

'I'm coming over! We're both coming over, Ted and me, right now! Ted's taken the morning off work. We'll be with you in half an hour. That's what friends are for!'

'Madge, that's kind of you, but I'm fine—' Joan stopped. She realized Madge had hung up.

'Shit!' she said.

Then she sniffed. She suddenly noticed a strange smell. But it was not that strange. It was a smell she knew only too well.

It was cigar smoke, again.

It was the smell of Victor's cigars. It was getting stronger by the second. 'Can you smell it?' she said to Don.

'Smell what?'

Joan closed her eyes. 'You must be able to smell it!'

'I can't smell anything.'

'Jesus, Don, what's the matter with you?'

'What's the matter with *me*?' He stared at her in shock. 'You need to calm down.'

'I AM CALM!' she yelled at him. 'Just take all the stuff from last night and GO! GET OUT OF HERE. TED AND MADGE ARE COMING. GO!'

Don took all the empty bags and tools and loaded them into his van, which was once again backed up against the garage door. 'I'll call you later, my love,' he said.

But Joan did not hear him. She was in the shower, scrubbing her body and washing her hair.

Stepping out, she dried herself, then towel-dried her hair. She sat down at her dressing table in front of the bed and began to apply some make-up. As she was putting on her lipstick, something moved in the mirror.

She spun round.

Victor was standing in the doorway. He was smiling at her.

Not the fat, balding Victor with a comb-over. It was the young, handsome Victor that she had married. Young, slim Victor, with his smooth brown hair and his gorgeous smile.

'I'm sorry,' she said. 'I – I don't know what happened. To us. Right?'

The doorbell rang.

Victor vanished.

She ran down the stairs and opened the front door. Her hair was a mess, her make-up only half on. Madge and Ted stood there. Each of them gave her a big hug.

'You poor thing!' Madge said.

'So where's the old bugger gone, then?' said Ted. 'Chopped him up, have you, and buried him under the kitchen floor?'

'That's not funny, Ted!' Madge chided.

'I've thought about doing that to Madge a few times, I don't mind telling you!' Ted said.

'Oooh, you're so wicked!' Madge replied. 'Don't listen to him! Come on, love, let's get the kettle on. Tell us all about it.'

Joan put the kettle on and told them all about it. She just left out the bit about her and Don being lovers, and the bit about killing Victor, and the bit about burying him under the garage floor. Apart from that, she told them pretty much everything.

Which was nothing.

Ted summed it up. 'So, he got made redundant and was depressed?'

'Yes,' Joan said.

'Why didn't the stupid bugger tell us?' Ted asked.

Joan shrugged. 'Pride, I suppose.'

'Pride comes before the fall,' Madge said, unhelpfully.

'I'll give him a piece of my mind when I see him,' Ted said. 'Making a drama out of this! Losing your job is nothing these days. I could lose mine at any time.'

'You'd better not,' Madge warned him sharply.

'Just teasing!' Ted laughed, and kissed her.

'He's such a tease, Ted is!' Madge said.

Joan could not wait for them to leave. She really did not want them to be here, in her kitchen, in her home, gobbling down her biscuits and her coffee. She did not want them doing all their lovey-dovey stuff.

But they stayed, and they stayed, and they stayed. By midday, she was almost out of coffee and biscuits. She was almost out of anything to say.

'He'll be back,' Madge said.

'He will, you'll see,' Ted said.

'He's not the suicidal type,' Madge added.

'No, not the suicidal type at all,' Ted agreed.

Then the doorbell rang.

Joan opened it without checking through the window. Standing on the doorstep were two men in suits.

One introduced himself as Detective Sergeant Mick Brett. The other was Detective Constable Paul Badger. They asked if they could come in.

Chapter Twenty

Joan introduced Ted and Madge to the two detectives. 'They are just leaving,' she added.

Madge said she would call this evening, to see how she was.

Ted gave her a kiss and told her not to worry. 'Victor will be back,' he said.

'He will, he'll be back,' Madge added.

'I'd offer you coffee, but I've run out of milk,' Joan said to the detectives. 'I can give you black, if you'd like?'

'I'm fine, thank you, Mrs Smiley,' DS Brett said. He was a big man, with a shaven head that was shaped like a rugby ball.

'I'm fine too,' DC Badger said. He looked quite jolly, she thought. He was all smiles, with a boyish face and a modern haircut.

She sat them down on the lounge sofa. She

cleared away the tray of coffee cups and plates covered in biscuit crumbs. 'Can't even offer you a biscuit,' she apologized loudly from the kitchen. 'If you'd come this evening, I'd have had a new packet.'

Then she walked back in and sat down opposite the two men.

'Uniform Division has asked CID to take over the investigation into your missing husband, Mrs Smiley,' Detective Sergeant Brett said.

'Oh, I see. That's good, isn't it?'

'Well,' he answered, 'it's good in the sense that Uniform are concerned about Mr Smiley's safety.'

Joan made a show of pressing a finger against each eye in turn, then sniffing. 'I'm so worried,' she said. 'I'm so worried about my poor darling Victor. I'm at my wits' end.'

DS Brett pulled out his notebook. 'There are a few things that we need to discuss with you, Mrs Smiley.'

'Of course,' she said.

'The first is your husband's mobile phone. When you filed a Missing Persons Report at

Brighton Police Station yesterday, you said that you had rung his number many times since Monday evening. Do you remember saying that?'

Joan's mouth suddenly felt dry. 'Yes, yes, I do.'

'Well, we have obtained his mobile phone records from Vodafone. There is only one call from your mobile number to his. There is none from your landline. This call was yesterday evening. Can you explain that?'

Her head was spinning. She felt clammy all over. Then her eyes darted to the open doorway. She was certain she had seen something moving. Both police officers turned and looked in the same direction too. But there was nothing there.

'Well,' she said. 'The thing is—' She fell silent for a moment. Then she went on: 'You see, there must be a mistake. I've called him – I don't know – I don't know how many times. The phone company must have made a mistake.'

DC Badger was looking back at the doorway again now. She resisted the temptation to look as well. She did not want to appear anxious. Then, a little distracted, he turned back to her. 'Is there anyone else in the house at the moment, Mrs Smiley?'

She shook her head. 'No.'

'Are you certain?'

'Yes, there's no one.' She shot another glance at the doorway.

'Does he have another mobile phone, with a different number, perhaps, that you've been calling?'

Again she was silent for a moment, trying to think what to say. Her stomach felt as if it was plunging down a lift shaft. 'No, there's no other phone. I just don't understand this.'

DS Brett made a note on his pad, then flipped back a page. 'When the two uniformed police officers were here last night, they asked you about a white van that was parked in your driveway. You told them it belonged to your plumber. Is that correct?'

Her stomach felt as if it was plunging even faster now. She was starting to feel that everything was coming undone around her. 'It belongs to my plumber, yes.'

The detective sergeant studied his notes for a moment. 'The van belongs to a business called Mile Oak Electrical Supplies. They do plumbing as well, do they?'

'I believe my plumber borrowed the van,' she said in a trembling voice. 'That's why he was working late, of course. His van had broken down, so he came late.'

She felt the sweat popping on her brow. Relief surged through her. Her lie had sounded okay, she thought.

The DS made another note, then glanced at his colleague and back at Joan. 'Right. Mrs Smiley, I'm afraid the next thing I have to ask may be a little distressing for you.' He fell silent and glanced at his colleague again. DC Badger looked at him with a serious expression.

'Oh?' Joan said.

The DS went on, 'Were you aware that your husband, Victor, was having an affair? Did you know that he was planning to leave you?' Both men were studying her face carefully.

Joan sat very still, in shock. After some moments, she said, 'An affair? My Victor?' She shook her head. 'I don't believe it! Not Victor. I mean, who on earth would—?'

She stopped in mid-sentence.

DC Badger was looking at the doorway again.

'Do go on,' the DS said.

'I'm sorry, I just don't believe that.'

'Does the name Kamila Walczak mean anything to you?'

'Should it?'

'She rang your husband's mobile number last night.'

'So?'

'She withheld her number and left no message.'

Now Joan remembered the call that had come in on Victor's phone. There had been no number in the display and no message. Was that her?

She said, a little acidly, 'Well, I've never heard of her. Who is she?'

'She works as a *hostess* at a club in Brighton,' the detective sergeant said.

'The lady is mistaken. Victor doesn't go to clubs.'

The two detectives looked at each other before Brett spoke again. 'I don't know how best to put this to you, Mrs Smiley. To be blunt, it is a sex club. This young lady is a sex worker.'

'A prostitute? Is that what you mean? A *call girl*? A *tart*?'

'I'm afraid so, yes.'

'My Victor seeing a prostitute? He couldn't! For a start, where would he have got the money?'

'I can't answer that for you, Mrs Smiley. All I can tell you is that Miss Walczak came in to see us just a short while ago. She is very upset. She told us that she and your husband were planning to start a new life together.'

Joan shook her head. 'She's made a mistake. Mistaken identity.'

DC Badger was looking at the doorway again. Then he said, 'We showed her a photograph of your husband. She identified him, without any doubt.'

'Maybe she's hiding something,' Joan said. 'Could she have harmed Victor, do you think?'

'That will certainly be one of our lines of inquiry.'

'My Victor with a hooker? I can't believe it! I – I just can't believe it.'

'We're mentioning it, Mrs Smiley, because it is possible he has other lady friends as well. He could perhaps be with one of those at the moment.'

'ABSOLUTELY NOT!' Joan said loudly. The shock of this news was still spinning in her head. Victor seeing a prostitute. How many years had this been going on? Bastard! How dare he?

'You are really sure, Mrs Smiley?' the constable asked.

Something in his voice made her think for a moment. Suddenly, Joan realized that she was being given a gift by the police! She had the perfect reason for Victor to disappear. He had another woman.

She put on a false smile and dabbed her eyes with her fingers again. 'How well do we know anyone? I thought I knew Victor. I thought he was very happy. Clearly, I must have been wrong if he's gone running off to tarts. Yes, you're right, there could be others. There could be loads! Maybe even in other countries? No

110

wonder he kept me so short of money!'

'Did you check to see if he had taken his passport with him, by any chance?' DS Brett asked.

She nodded and then lied again. 'Yes, actually I did. He had taken it. Yes, it was gone from his desk! It was one of the first things I checked.'

'Why didn't you mention that in your report to PCSO Watts?'

'I was in such a state,' she said. 'I must have forgotten! Can you imagine what it is like to lose the person you love?'

She began to sob.

The detectives left a short while later. They seemed to spend a long time sitting in their silver Ford Focus outside, talking to each other. Finally, they drove off.

It was ten to one. Joan needed to hurry or she would be late for work. Instead, she stood still for some minutes, staring out of the window. Anger was boiling inside her. Victor had cheated on her. He had been going to a tart! For how long? How much money had he spent on this tart?

She marched over to the internal door to the garage and unlocked it. She opened it and stared down at the smooth cement screed covering the floor.

'YOU BASTARD!' she shouted.

Chapter Twenty-One

DS Brett drove the Focus. They were heading back towards the police station. DC Badger stared at the photograph of Victor Smiley on his lap. It was the one that had been circulated, and was being put on Missing Persons posters in police stations around the county.

'It didn't feel right to me. What about you?' the detective sergeant said.

'She was nervous about something. She kept looking at the doorway,' Badger replied. 'The feeling I got is that she has something to hide. If she's reported her husband missing, and he was lurking in the doorway all the time we were there, someone's having a laugh at us.'

'So what do you think she's playing at?' the DS asked him.

'Could it be an insurance scam? We should

check to see if there are any life insurance policies on him. There was a couple who did that a while ago. What were they called? Darwin. The husband faked his death in a canoe and they got a life insurance payout. He hid in the attic for five years.'

'Why didn't you ask her about it?'

'I didn't want her to think I was suspicious. She said there was no one in the house, right?'

Brett nodded. 'So you think her husband might be alive and well, and hiding in the house?'

'Possibly, chief. We know she's been lying to us about the phone. What else has she been lying about?'

'I see where you're coming from,' DS Brett said.

Chapter Twenty-Two

Shortly after six o'clock that evening, Joan edged the purple Astra into her driveway and stopped in front of the garage. She had two bottles of wine in the boot, which she had bought from the supermarket. She also had several packets of biscuits, some prawn cocktails at the end of their best-before dates, and two steaks.

Don was coming over. He said they had to drink a toast. She wasn't really keen to see him at the moment, but she didn't want to be alone in the house. She had decided to make him supper. It was strange, she thought, that he had exactly the same taste in food as Victor. She had read that when a man leaves his wife for a younger model, he often chooses someone who looks like his wife. Maybe a woman chooses a new man who has the same tastes as her old one?

She was thinking about all the police she had seen in the past couple of days. She was trying to work out if she had said the right things. It had been tricky. But she felt she had kept calm. She would talk through it all with Don tonight. They should check to see what they had missed and what they needed to do.

As she got out of the car in the fading light, a strong wind was blowing. She noticed several of her neighbours' curtains twitching. They were watching her. She decided it would be safest to put the car in the garage, so they would not see her unloading the bottles.

Don had told her not to drive on the new garage floor for a few days to let it harden. But it seemed pretty hard now.

She lifted the door, stared at the smooth cement and tested it with her feet. It was fine! Hard as rock!

She drove in and pulled the door shut behind her. It closed with a clang that seemed to echo for ever. Then she carried everything through into the kitchen. She put the wine straight into the fridge. Then she switched on the television and all the lights in the house, because she was nervous that Victor's ghost might suddenly appear again. After that she went upstairs to the bedroom and stepped out of her work clothes. She freshened up, sprayed herself with the perfume that Don liked, and laid out her short black cocktail dress on the bed.

At that moment, the front doorbell rang.

She frowned. It was only a quarter past six. Don wasn't due until seven.

Dressed only in her knickers and bra, she hurried into Victor's den and looked out of the window. Her throat tightened. There were two marked police cars out in the street, and a white van with police markings on it. The two detectives who had come round earlier were standing at the front door.

The bell rang again.

'Coming!' she called out, trying not to sound anxious.

She took a deep breath and hastily put her work clothes back on. Then she hurried back downstairs.

As she opened the door, Detective Sergeant

Brett held up a sheet of paper. A group of police officers in yellow jackets stood behind him and Detective Constable Badger.

'Mrs Smiley,' DS Brett said, 'we have a search warrant for your house.' He showed it to her.

She was shaking as she looked at it, but it was just a blur. 'A search warrant?'

'Yes, madam.'

'What is this about?'

Half a dozen policemen walked past her, followed by the two detectives.

'Would anyone like tea or coffee?' she asked. Then she added, 'I've got some biscuits now!'

No one replied. Suddenly, every room in the house seemed to have a police officer in it.

'Expecting company, are you?' DS Brett said, looking at the two raw steaks on the kitchen drainer.

'Just me and the cat,' she said.

'Lucky cat. Prime rib steak!' he replied, snapping on a pair of latex gloves.

'He's very fussy,' she answered lamely.

'Have a seat,' DS Brett said, pointing to a kitchen chair. 'We're going to be a while.'

* * *

118

Upstairs, DC Badger pushed open a door into a tiny room that looked like a spare bedroom. There was a cold draught, and a strong smell of fresh paint. There was also a fainter smell of bitter almonds, which he did not notice.

He switched on the light. The room looked like it had been freshly decorated. The walls were painted a deep blue colour. A crisp white blind flapped in the wind that was howling in through the wide-open window. He noticed a single bed with a cream candlewick counter-pane. The bed was made up but not slept in. There was a bedside table with a lamp, and a small chest of drawers. He began to check through them.

Downstairs in the kitchen, Joan stared blankly at an episode of *Poirot* on the television. She switched channels. It was another Agatha Christie, this time a Miss Marple. Hastily, she switched again. John Thaw, in *Morse*, was standing at a grave being opened. She switched once more. Now it was the actor Basil Rathbone playing Sherlock Holmes.

'Stop it, you bastard!' she mouthed silently.

She switched to BBC 1. It should be the end of the six o'clock news.

Instead, she saw Victor's face smiling out at her from the screen. She was about to change channels again when she heard the voice of a newscaster saying, 'Sussex Police are gravely worried about Victor Smiley, a diabetic who has not been seen for several days.'

She switched the television off.

Her heart was crashing around inside her chest.

Moments later, DC Badger entered the kitchen still wearing the latex gloves and holding a small, dark-red booklet. 'This appears to be your husband's passport. I found it in a desk in the front bedroom, which I presume is your husband's office.'

'Well done!' she said. 'What a relief! I searched everywhere for it.'

'Not hard enough,' he said.

Before she had time to reply, another officer came in. He was wearing a black vest with the letters POLSA on a badge on his chest. He was holding Victor's mobile phone. 'This appears to be your husband's mobile phone, Mrs

Smiley. I just checked the number.'

'Amazing! Where did you find it?'

'In a drawer in the hall table.'

'I – I looked there,' she said quietly.

'Not hard enough?' he said.

'No,' she agreed. 'Well done!'

DC Badger was staring at her. She felt her innards squirming. It was as if her intestines had turned into restless snakes.

Then Detective Sergeant Brett came back into the kitchen. 'We'd like to move the Vauxhall Astra out of the garage. Do you have the keys, please?'

They were in front of her, on the kitchen table, beside the carrier bag containing the prawn cocktails.

'I think my husband may have them with him,' she said. Then she saw the detective looking at them. 'Ah! No. What a surprise! Here they are!'

'What a surprise,' he said.

She stood by the internal door to the garage and watched the DS open the swing door. He reversed the car out. Joan stared in shock at what she saw.

The cement had sunk where the wheels of the car had been. A mound had risen in the centre of it. It was like a fat pot-belly sticking up through the floor. It was like Victor's belly. Cracked cement lay all along it and on either side of it.

She watched in dismay as four police officers appeared with shovels. A fifth officer had a pick-axe. They removed their yellow jackets and began to dig.

Suddenly, she heard a humming sound in her ears. The *Dam Busters* theme tune. It was Victor's favourite sodding tune.

It was the tune he always hummed when he was happy.

He continued to hum it throughout the next hour as she stood and watched.

He was humming it as the police steadily unearthed him. Bit by bit by bit.

Chapter Twenty-Three

Four days later, at six o'clock on Sunday evening, Joan was released on police bail. This was after three nights in custody and an endless series of interviews with different detectives.

She took a taxi home. It was not Don's taxi, of course. He had not been so lucky. He was remanded in custody, charged with Victor's murder.

Joan felt pretty pleased with how she had handled it all. She had given a performance worthy of an Oscar! The detectives seemed to believe her version of events. She told them that Victor had come home and had found Don there. He had attacked Don, and Don had hit him with a hammer. Then Don had threatened to tell the police that she had killed him, unless she kept quiet.

Don had buried him under the garage floor. That bit of the story was partly true, at least.

It had seemed quite true to the police. After they discovered Victor's body, they raided Don's house at dawn. There they found the bloodstained hammer in Don's toolbox, with his fingerprints on it.

Her solicitor told her that she was still in trouble. It was almost certain that she would be charged as an accessory to murder. This was likely to happen at some point in the next few weeks. However, he knew a good barrister. She would go to jail but, with luck, it would be a short sentence if the jury believed her story. Her solicitor could see no reason why they would not.

But for now, at least, she was free.

There were plenty of other men in the world, she thought, as she let herself in through the front door. It seemed likely that Don was going to be locked away for life. Well, too bad for him! There were dating agencies she could sign up to, dancing classes she could join. But the biggest joy of all was that there was no more Victor.

If his damned ghost persisted, she would call in a medium to get rid of him!

In any case, she planned to sell the house. There were too many memories. She had never liked this place anyway, not really. It had always been just a house, to her. It had never been a *home*.

As she went inside, it seemed even less of a home than ever. The police had made a right mess of it during these past days. They had pulled up carpets and floorboards, and punched holes in some of the walls. They had dug up parts of the garden to look for the murder weapon, before they found it at Don's.

She made straight for the fridge and poured herself a glass of wine, filling it right to the brim. She downed it in two gulps, filled it again, and did the same. Then she filled it a third time, emptying the bottle. She was now more than a little bit drunk. She said loudly and boldly, 'Victor, if you are still here, you can just sod off!'

She stared at the doorway. She looked into

the empty hall. She was not focusing very well.

Then she drank some more. 'Did you hear what I said, Victor?' Her voice was slurring.

Silence greeted her.

She burped, then said 'Sorry' to herself. She drained the rest of the glass.

It was a relief to be back in her own clothes after the horrible, badly fitting paper jumpsuit she'd been given to wear in her cell.

She was feeling hungry. And in need of more to drink. To her relief, there was one more bottle of wine in the fridge.

An hour later, Joan was very drunk. She staggered upstairs to her bedroom. She undressed and brushed her teeth, then fell into bed. The sheets and pillows smelled of Victor, but she was too drunk to care. Her eyes closed and she drifted into sleep.

Almost at once, she was woken by the loudest snoring she had ever heard. She balled her hand into a fist, as she used to do most nights, and thumped Victor, hard. But her hand just thudded into the empty mattress on Victor's side of the bed.

The snoring continued. It was getting louder. Louder still.

Suddenly, she was terrified. She snapped on the light.

Nothing. Silence.

She must have dreamed it, she thought, turning off the light again.

Instantly, she heard the snoring again.

She snapped the light back on and the snoring stopped. For some minutes she lay still, her heart pounding. 'Okay,' she said. 'I get the message! I'm going to my nice, newly decorated room. You can snore your sodding heart out!'

Wrapping the entire duvet around herself, she padded out of the bedroom. She slammed the door behind her, went across the landing into the little spare room, and slammed that door behind her too. The window was still wide open so she closed it, then she shut the new blind.

She switched off the bedside light.

'So thoughtful of you, Victor, to go to such trouble with this room,' she murmured as she snuggled down.

There was a faint smell of almonds. It was a nice smell, she thought. Much nicer than the smell of Victor.

Slowly, steadily, she drifted into sleep. A very deep sleep.

Bit by bit by bit.

DEAD SIMPLE

FOUR BODIES. ONE SUSPECT.
NO TRACE.

It was meant to be a harmless stag night prank. A few hours later four of his best friends are dead and Michael Harrison has disappeared.

With only three days to the wedding, Detective Superintendent Grace – a man haunted by the shadow of his own missing wife – is contacted by Michael's beautiful, distraught fiancée, Ashley Harper.

Grace discovers that the one man who ought to know Michael Harrison's whereabouts is saying nothing. But then he has a lot to gain – more than anyone realizes. For one man's disaster is another man's fortune . . . Dead simple . . .

'A brilliant idea, superbly crafted. A terrific page-turner'   James Herbert

Read on for an extract from *Dead Simple*, the first novel in Peter James' number one bestselling Roy Grace series . . .

Chapter One

So far, apart from just a couple of hitches, Plan A was working out fine. Which was fortunate, since they didn't really have a Plan B.

At 8.30 on a late May evening, they'd banked on having some daylight. There had been plenty of the stuff this time yesterday, when four of them had made the same journey, taking with them an empty coffin and four shovels. But now, as the green Transit van sped along the Sussex country road, misty rain was falling from a sky the colour of a fogged negative.

'Are we nearly there yet?' said Josh in the back, mimicking a child.

'The great Um Ga says, "Wherever I go there I am," responded Robbo, who was driving, and was slightly less drunk than the rest of them.

With three pubs notched up already in the past hour and a half, and four more on the itinerary, he was sticking to shandy. At least, that had been his intention; but he'd managed to slip down a couple of pints of pure Harvey's bitter – to clear his head for the task of driving, he'd said.

'So we are there!' said Josh.

'Always have been.'

A deer warning sign flitted from the darkness then was gone, as the headlights skimmed glossy black-top macadam stretching ahead into the forested distance. Then they passed a small white cottage.

Michael, lolling on a tartan rug on the floor in the back of the van, head wedged between the arms of a wheel-wrench for a pillow, was feeling very pleasantly woozy. 'I sh'ink I need another a drink,' he slurred.

If he'd had his wits about him, he might have sensed, from the expressions of his friends, that something was not quite right. Never usually much of a heavy drinker, tonight he'd parked his brains in the dregs of more empty pint glasses and vodka chasers than he could remember downing, in more pubs than had been sensible to visit.

Of the six of them who had been muckers together since way back into their early teens, Michael Harrison had always been the natural leader. If, as they say, the secret of life is to choose your parents wisely, Michael had ticked plenty of the right boxes. He had inherited his mother's fair good looks and his father's charm and entrepreneurial spirit, but without any of the self-destruct genes that had eventually ruined the man.

From the age of twelve, when Tom Harrison had gassed himself in the garage of the family home, leaving behind a trail of debtors, Michael had grown up fast, helping his mother make ends meet by doing a paper round, then when he was older by taking labouring jobs in his holidays. He grew up with an appreciation of how hard it was to make money – and how easy to fritter it.

Now, at twenty-eight, he was smart, a decent human being, and a natural leader of the pack. If he had flaws, it was that he was too trusting and on occasions, too much of a prankster. And tonight that latter chicken was coming home to roost. Big time.

But at this moment he had no idea of that.

He drifted back again into a blissful stupor, thinking only happy thoughts, mostly about his fiancée, Ashley. Life was good. His mother was dating a nice guy, his kid brother had just got into university, his kid sister Carly was backpacking in Australia on a gap year, and his business was going incredibly well. But best of all, in three days time he was going to be marrying the woman he loved. And adored. His soul mate.

Ashley.

He hadn't noticed the shovel that rattled on every bump in the road, as the wheels drummed below on the sodden tarmac, and the rain pattered down above him on the roof. And he didn't clock a thing in the expressions of his two friends riding along with him in the back, who were swaying and singing tunelessly to an oldie, Rod Stewart's 'Sailing', on the crackly radio up front. A leaky fuel can filled the van with the stench of petrol.

'I love her,' Michael slurred. 'I sh'love Ashley.'

'She's a great lady,' Robbo said, turning his head from the wheel, sucking up to him as he always did. That was in his nature. Awkward with women, a bit clumsy, a florid face, lank hair, beer belly straining the weave of his T-shirt, Robbo hung to the coat tails of this bunch by always trying to make himself needed. And tonight, for a change, he actually *was* needed.

'She is.'

'Coming up,' warned Luke.

Robbo braked as they approached the turn-off and winked in the darkness of the cab at Luke seated next to him. The wipers clumped steadily, smearing the rain across the wind-screen.

'I mean, like I really love her. Sh'now what I mean?'

'We know what you mean,' Pete said.

Josh, leaning back against the driver's seat, one arm around Pete, swigged some beer, then passed the bottle down to Michael. Froth rose from the neck as the van braked sharply. He belched. ''Scuse me.'

'What the hell does Ashley see in you?' Josh said.

'My dick.'

'So it's not your money? Or your looks? Or your charm?'

'That too, Josh, but mostly my dick.'

The van lurched as it made the sharp right turn, rattling over a cattle grid, almost immediately followed by a second one, and onto the dirt track. Robbo, peering through the misted glass, picking out the deep ruts, swung the wheel. A rabbit sprinted ahead of them, then shot into some undergrowth. The headlights veered right then left, fleetingly colouring the dense conifers that lined the track, before they vanished into darkness in the rear-view mirror. As Robbo changed down a gear, Michael's voice changed, his bravado suddenly tinged, very faintly, with anxiety.

'Where we going?'

'To another pub.'

'OK. Great.' Then a moment later, 'Promised Ashley I shwouldn't – wouldn't – drink too much.'

'See,' Pete said, 'you're not even married and she's laying down rules. You're still a free man. For just three more days.'

'Three and a half,' Robbo added, helpfully.

'You haven't arranged any girls?' Michael said.

'Feeling horny?' Robbo asked.

'I'm staying faithful.'

'We're making sure of that.'

'Bastards!'

The van lurched to a halt, reversed a short distance, then made another right turn. Then it stopped again, and Robbo killed the engine – and Rod Stewart with it. *'Arrivé!'* he said. 'Next watering hole! The Undertaker's Arms!'

'I'd prefer the Naked Thai Girl's Legs,' Michael said.

'She's here too.'

Someone opened the rear door of the van, Michael wasn't sure who. Invisible hands took hold of his ankles. Robbo took one of his arms, and Luke the other.

'Hey!'

'You're a heavy bastard!' Luke said.

Moments later Michael thumped down, in his favourite sports jacket and best jeans (not the wisest choice for your stag night, a dim voice in his head was telling him) onto sodden earth, in pitch darkness which was pricked only by the red tail lights of the van and the white beam of a flashlight. Hardening rain stung his eyes and matted his hair to his forehead.

'My – closhes—'

Moments later, his arms yanked almost clear of their sockets, he was hoisted in the air, then dumped down into something dry and lined with white satin that pressed in on either side of him.

'Hey!' he said again.

Four drunken, grinning shadowy faces leered down at him. A magazine was pushed into his hands. In the beam of the flashlight he caught a blurry glimpse of a naked redhead with gargantuan breasts. A bottle of whisky, a small flashlight, switched on, and a walkie-talkie were placed on his stomach.

'What's—?'

A piece of foul-tasting rubber tubing was pushing into his mouth. As Michael spat it out, he heard a scraping sound, then suddenly something blotted the faces out. And blotted all the sound out. His nostrils filled with smells of wood, new cloth and glue. For an instant he felt warm and snug. Then a flash of panic.

'Hey, guys – what—'

Robbo picked up a screwdriver, as Pete shone the flashlight down on the teak coffin.

'You're not screwing it down?' Luke said.

'Absolutely!' Pete said.

'Do you think we should?'

'He'll be fine,' Robbo said. 'He's got the breathing tube!'

'I really don't think we should screw it down!'

''Course we do – otherwise he'll be able to get out!'

'Hey—' Michael said.

But no one could hear him now. And he could hear nothing except a faint scratching sound above him.

Robbo worked on each of the four screws in turn. It was a top-of-the-range hand-tooled teak coffin with embossed brass handles, borrowed from his uncle's funeral parlour, where, after a couple of career U-turns, he was now employed as an apprentice embalmer. Good, solid brass screws. They went in easily.

Michael looked upwards, his nose almost

touching the lid. In the beam of the flashlight, ivory-white satin encased him. He kicked out with his legs, but they had nowhere to travel. He tried to push his arms out. But they had nowhere to go, either.

Sobering for a few moments, he suddenly realized what he was lying in.

'Hey, hey, listen, you know – hey – I'm claustrophobic – this is not funny! Hey!' His voice came back at him, strangely muffled.

Pete opened the door, leaned into the cab, and switched on the headlights. A couple of metres in front of them was the grave they had dug yesterday, the earth piled to one side, tapes already in place. A large sheet of corrugated iron and two of the spades they had used lay close by.

The four friends walked to the edge and peered down. All of them were suddenly aware that nothing in life is ever quite as it seems when you are planning it. This hole right now looked deeper, darker, more like – well – a grave, actually.

The beam of the flashlight shimmered at the bottom.

'There's water,' Josh said.

'Just a bit of rainwater,' Robbo said.

Josh frowned. 'There's too much, that's not rainwater. We must have hit the water table.'

'Shit,' Pete said. A BMW salesman, he always looked the part, on duty or off. Spiky haircut, sharp suit, always confident. But not quite so confident now.

'It's nothing,' Robbo said. 'Just a couple of inches.'

'Did we really dig it this deep?' said Luke, a freshly qualified solicitor, recently married, not quite ready to shrug off his youth, but starting to accept life's responsibilities.

'It's a grave, isn't it?' said Robbo. 'We decided on a grave.'

Josh squinted up at the worsening rain. 'What if the water rises?

'Shit, man,' Robbo said. 'We dug it yesterday, it's taken twenty-four hours for just a couple of inches. Nothing to worry about.'

Josh nodded, thoughtfully. 'But what if we can't get him back out?'

'Course we can get him out,' Robbo said. 'We just unscrew the lid.'

'Let's just get on with it,' Luke said. 'OK?'

'He bloody deserves it,' Pete reassured his mates. 'Remember what he did on your stag night, Luke?'

Luke would never forget. Waking from an alcoholic stupor to find himself on a bunk on the overnight sleeper to Edinburgh. Arriving forty minutes late at the altar the next afternoon as a result.

Pete would never forget, either. The weekend before his wedding, he'd found himself in frilly lace underwear, a dildo strapped to his waist, manacled to the Clifton Gorge suspension bridge, before being rescued by the fire brigade. Both pranks had been Michael's idea.

'Typical of Mark,' Pete said. 'Jammy bastard. He's the one who organized this and now he isn't bloody here . . .'

'He's coming. He'll be at the next pub, he knows the itinerary.'

'Oh yes?'

'He rang, he's on his way.'

'Fogbound in Leeds. Great!' Robbo said.

'He'll be at the Royal Oak by the time we get there.'

'Jammy bastard,' Luke said. 'He's missing out on all the hard work.'

'And the *fun*!' Pete reminded him.

'This is fun?' Luke said. 'Standing in the middle of a sodding forest in the pissing rain? Fun? God, you're sad! He'd fucking better turn up to help us get Michael back out.'

They hefted the coffin up in the air, staggered forward with it to the edge of the grave and dumped it down, hard, over the tapes. Then giggled at the muffled 'Ouch!' from within it.

There was a loud thump.

Michael banged his fist against the lid. 'Hey! Enough!'

Pete, who had the walkie-talkie in his coat pocket, pulled it out and switched it on. 'Testing!' he said. 'Testing!'

Inside the coffin, Pete's voice boomed out. 'Testing! Testing!'

'Joke over!'

'Relax, Michael!' Pete said. 'Enjoy!'

'You bastards! Let me out! I need a piss!'

Pete switched the walkie-talkie off and jammed it into the pocket of his Barbour jacket. 'So how does this work, exactly?'

'We lift the tapes,' Robbo said. 'One each end.'

Pete dug the walkie-talkie out and switched it on. 'We're getting this taped, Michael!' Then he switched it off again.

The four of them laughed. Then each picked up an end of tape and took up the slack.

'One . . . two . . . three!' Robbo counted.

'Fuck, this is heavy!' Luke said, taking the strain and lifting.

Slowly, jerkily, listing like a stricken ship, the coffin sank down into the deep hole.

When it reached the bottom they could barely see it in the darkness.

Pete held the flashlight. In the beam they could make out the breathing tube sticking limply out of the drinking-straw-sized hole that had been cut in the lid.

Robbo grabbed the walkie-talkie. 'Hey, Michael, your dick's sticking out. Are you enjoying the magazine?'

'OK, joke over. Now let me out!'

'We're off to a pole-dancing club. Too bad you can't join us!' Robbo switched off the radio before Michael could reply. Then, pocketing it, he picked up a spade and began shovelling earth over the edge of the grave and roared with laughter as it rattled down on the roof of the coffin.

With a loud *whoop* Pete grabbed another shovel and joined in. For some moments both of them worked hard until only a few bald patches of coffin showed through the earth. Then these were covered. Both of them continued, the drink fuelling their work into a frenzy, until there was a good couple of feet of earth piled on top of the coffin. The breathing tube barely showed above it.

'Hey!' Luke said. 'Hey, stop that! The more you shovel on the more we're going to have to dig back out again in two hours' time.'

'It's a grave!' Robbo said. 'That's what you do with a grave, you cover the coffin!'

Luke grabbed the spade from him. 'Enough!' he said, firmly. 'I want to spend the evening drinking, not bloody digging, OK?'

Robbo nodded, never wanting to upset anyone in the group. Pete, sweating heavily, threw his spade down. 'Don't think I'll take this up as a career,' he said.

They pulled the corrugated iron sheet over the top, then stood back in silence for some moments. Rain pinged on the metal.

'OK,' Pete said. 'We're outta here.'

Luke dug his hands into his coat pocket, dubiously. 'Are we really sure about this?'

'We agreed we were going to teach him a lesson,' Robbo said.

'What if he chokes on his vomit, or something?'

'He'll be fine, he's not that drunk,' Josh said. 'Let's go.'

Josh climbed into the rear of the van, and Luke shut the doors. Then Pete, Luke and Robbo squeezed into the front, and Robbo started the engine. They drove back down the track for half a mile, then made a right turn onto the main road.

Then he switched on the walkie-talkie. 'How you doing, Michael?'

'Guys, listen, I'm really not enjoying this joke.'

'Really?' Robbo said. 'We are!'

Luke took the radio. 'This is what's known as pure vanilla revenge, Michael!'

All four of them in the van roared with laughter. Now it was Josh's turn. 'Hey, Michael, we're going to this fantastic club, they have the most beautiful women, butt naked, sliding their bodies up and down poles. You're going to be really pissed you're missing out on this!'

Michael's voice slurred back, just a tad plaintive. 'Can we stop this now, please? I'm really not enjoying this.'

Through the windscreen Robbo could see roadworks ahead, with a green light. He accelerated.

Luke shouted over Josh's shoulder, 'Hey, Michael, just relax, we'll be back in a couple of hours!'

'What do you mean, *a couple of hours*?'

The light turned red. Not enough time to stop. Robbo accelerated even harder and shot through. 'Gimme the thing,' he said, grabbing the radio and steering one-handed around a long curve. He peered down in the ambient glow of the dash and hit the *talk* button.

'Hey, Michael—'

'ROBBO!' Luke's voice, screaming.

Headlights above them, coming straight at them.

Blinding them.

Then the blare of a horn, deep, heavy duty, ferocious.

'ROBBBBBBBBOOOOOOO!' screamed Luke.

Robbo stamped in panic on the brake pedal and dropped the walkie-talkie. The wheel yawed in his hands as he looked, desperately, for somewhere to go. Trees to his right, a JCB to his left, headlights burning through the windscreen, searing his eyes, coming at him out of the teeming rain, like a train.

Chapter Two

Michael, his head swimming, heard shouting, then a sharp *thud*, as if someone had dropped the walkie-talkie.

Then silence.

He pressed the *talk* button. 'Hello?'

Just empty static came back at him.

'Hello? Hey guys!'

Still nothing. He focused his eyes on the two-way radio. It was a stubby-looking thing, a hard, black plastic casing, with one short aerial and one longer one, the name '*Motorola*' embossed over the speaker grille. There was also an on–off switch, a volume control, a channel selector, and a tiny pinhead of a green light that was glowing brightly. Then he stared at the white satin that was inches from his eyes, fighting panic, starting to breathe faster and faster. He needed to pee, badly, going on desperately.

Where the hell was he? Where were Josh, Luke, Pete, Robbo? Standing around, giggling? Had the bastards really gone off to a club?

Then his panic subsided as the alcohol kicked back in again. His thoughts became leaden, muddled. His eyes closed and he was almost suckered into sleep.

Opening his eyes, the satin blurred into soft focus, as a roller wave of nausea suddenly swelled up inside him, threw him up in the air then dropped him down. Up again. Down again. He swallowed, closed his eye again, giddily, feeling the coffin drifting, swaying from side to side, floating. The need to pee was receding. Suddenly the nausea wasn't so bad any more. It was snug in here. Floating. Like being in a big bed!

His eyes closed and he sank like a stone into sleep.

Chapter Three

Roy Grace sat in the dark, in his ageing Alfa Romeo in the line of stationary traffic, rain drumming the roof, his fingers drumming the wheel, barely listening to the Dido CD that was playing. He felt tense. Impatient. Gloomy.

He felt like shit.

Tomorrow he was due to appear in court, and he knew he was in trouble.

He took a swig of bottled Evian water, replaced the cap and jammed the bottle back in the door pocket. 'Come on, come on!' he said, fingers tapping again, harder now. He was already forty minutes late for his date. He hated being late, always felt it was a sign of rudeness, as if you were making the statement, *my time's more important than yours, so I can keep you waiting . . .*

If he had left the office just one minute sooner he wouldn't have been late: someone else would have taken the call and the ram-raid on a jewellery shop in Brighton, by two punks who were high on God-knows-what, would have been a colleague's problem, not his. That was one of the occupational hazards of police work – villains didn't have the courtesy to keep to office hours.

He should not be going out tonight, he knew. Should have stayed home, preparing himself for tomorrow. Tugging out the bottle, he drank some more water. His mouth was dry, parched. Leaden butterflies flip-flopped in his belly.

Friends had pushed him into a handful of blind dates over the past few years, and each time he'd been a bag of nerves before he'd shown up. The nerves were even worse tonight, and, not having had a chance to shower and change, he felt uncomfortable about his appearance. All his detailed planning about what he was going to wear had gone out of the window, thanks to the two punks.

One of them had fired a sawn-off shotgun at an off-duty cop who had come too close to the jewellery shop – but luckily not quite close enough. Roy had seen, more times than he had needed, the effects of a 12-bore fired from a few feet at a human being. It could shear off a limb or punch a hole the size of a football through their chest. This cop, a detective called Bill Green who Grace knew – they had played rugger on the same team a few times – had been peppered from about thirty yards. At this distance the pellets could just about have brought down a pheasant or a rabbit, but not a fifteen-stone scrum prop in a leather jacket. Bill Green was relatively lucky – his jacket had shielded his body but he had several pellets embedded in his face, including one in his left eye.

By the time Grace had got to the scene, the punks were already in custody, after crashing and rolling their getaway Jeep. He was determined to stick them with an attempted murder charge on top of armed robbery. He hated the way more and more criminals were using guns in the UK – and forcing more and more police to have firearms to hand. In his father's day armed cops would have been unheard of. Now in some cities forces kept guns in the boots of their cars as routine. Grace wasn't naturally a vengeful person, but so far as he was concerned, anyone who fired a gun at a police officer – or at any innocent person – should be hanged.

The traffic still wasn't moving. He looked at the dash clock, at the rain falling, at the clock again, at the burning red tail lights of the car in front – the prat had his fogs on, almost dazzling him. Then he checked his watch, hoping the car clock might be wrong. But it wasn't. Ten whole minutes had passed and they hadn't moved an inch. Nor had any traffic come past from the opposite direction.

Shards of blue light flitted across his interior mirror and wing mirror. Then he heard a siren. A patrol car screamed past. Then an ambulance. Another patrol car, flat out, followed by two fire engines.

Shit. There had been road works when he'd come this way a couple of days ago, and he'd figured that was the reason for the delay. But now he realized it must be an accident, and fire engines meant it was a bad one.

Another fire engine went past. Then another ambulance, twos-and-blues full on. Followed by a rescue truck.

He looked at the clock again: 9.15 p.m. He should have picked her up three-quarters of an hour ago, in Tunbridge Wells, which was still a good twenty minutes away without this hold-up.

Terry Miller, a newly divorced Detective Inspector in Grace's division, had been regaling him with boasts about his conquests from a couple of internet dating sites and urging Grace to sign up. Roy had resisted, then, when he started finding suggestive emails in his inbox from different women, found out to his fury that Terry Miller had signed him up to a site called U-Date without telling him.

He still had no idea what had prompted him to actually respond to one of the emails. Loneliness? Curiosity? Lust? He wasn't sure. For the past eight years he had got through life just by going steadily from day to day. Some days he tried to forget, other days he felt guilty for not remembering.

Sandy.

Now he was suddenly feeling guilty for going on this date.

She looked gorgeous – from her photo, at any rate. He liked her name, too. Claudine. French-sounding, it had something exotic. Her picture was hot! Amber hair, seriously pretty face, tight blouse showing a weapons-grade bust, sitting on the edge of a bed with a miniskirt pulled high enough to show she was wearing lace-topped holdups and *might* not be wearing knickers.

They'd had just one phone conversation, in which she had practically seduced him down the line. A bunch of flowers he'd bought at a petrol station lay on the passenger seat beside him. Red roses – corny, he knew, but that was the old-fashioned romantic in him. People were right, he did need to move on, somehow. He could count the dates he'd had in the past eight and three-quarter years on just one hand. He simply could not accept there might be another Miss Right out there. That there could ever be anyone who matched up to Sandy.

Maybe tonight that feeling would change?

Claudine Lamont. Nice name, nice voice.

Turn those sodding fog lamps off!

He smelled the sweet scent of the flowers. Hoped he smelled OK, too.

In the ambient glow from the Alfa's dash and the tail lights of the car in front, he stared up at the mirror, unsure what he expected to see. Sadness stared back at him.

You have to move on.

He swallowed more water. Yup.

In just over two months he would be thirty-nine. In just over two months also another anniversary loomed. On 26 July Sandy would have been gone for nine years. Vanished into thin air, on his thirtieth birthday. No note. All her belongings still in the house except for her handbag.

After seven years you could have someone declared legally dead. His mother, in her hospice bed, days before she passed away from cancer, his sister, his closest friends, his shrink, all of them told him he should do that.

No way.

John Lennon had said, 'Life is what happens to you when you're busy making other plans.' That sure as hell was true.

By thirty-six he had always assumed Sandy and he would have had a family. Three kids had always been his dream, ideally two boys and a girl, and his weekends would be spent doing stuff with them. Family holidays. Going to the beach. Out on day trips to fun places. Playing ball games. Fixing things. Helping them at nights with homework. Bathing them. All the comfortable stuff he'd done with his own parents.

Instead he was consumed with an inner turbulence that rarely left him, even when it allowed him to sleep. Was she alive or dead? He'd spent eight years and ten months trying to find out and was still no nearer to the truth than when he had started.

Outside of work, life was a void. He'd been unable – or unwilling – to attempt another relationship. Every date he'd been on was a disaster. It seemed at times that his only constant companion in his life was his goldfish, Marlon. He'd won the fish by target shooting at a fairground, nine years ago, and it had eaten all his subsequent attempts to provide it with a companion. Marlon was a surly, antisocial creature. Probably why they liked each other, Roy reflected. They were two of a kind.

Sometimes he wished he wasn't a policeman, that he did some less demanding job where he could switch off at five o'clock, go to the pub and then home, put his feet up in front of the telly. Normal life. But he couldn't help it. There was some stubbornness or determination gene – or bunch of genes – inside him – and his father before him – that had driven him relentlessly throughout his life to pursue facts, to pursue the truth. It was those genes that had brought him up through the ranks, to his relatively early promotion to Detective Superintendent. But they hadn't brought him any peace of mind.

His face stared back at him again from the mirror. Grace grimaced at his reflection, at his hair cropped short, to little more than a light fuzz, at his nose, squashed and kinked after being broken in a scrap when he'd been a beat copper, which gave him the appearance of a retired prize fighter.

On their first date, Sandy had told him he had eyes like Paul Newman. He'd liked that a lot. It was one of a million things he had liked about her. The fact that she had loved everything about him, unconditionally.

Roy Grace knew that he was physically fairly unimpressive. At five foot, ten inches, he had been just two inches over the minimum height restriction when he'd joined the police, nineteen years back. But despite his love of booze, and an on–off battle with cigarettes, through hard work at the police gym he had developed a powerful physique, and had kept in shape, running twenty miles a week, and still playing the occasional game of rugger – usually on the wing.

Nine-twenty.

Bloody hell.

He seriously did not want a late night. Did not need one. Could not afford one. He was in court tomorrow, and needed to bank a full night's sleep. The whole thought of the cross-examination that awaited him pressed all kinds of bad buttons inside him.

A pool of light suddenly flooded down from above him, and he heard the clattering din of a helicopter. After a moment the light moved forward, and he saw the helicopter descending.

He dialled a number on his mobile. It was answered almost immediately.

'Hi, it's Detective Superintendent Grace speaking. I'm sitting in a traffic jam on the A26 south of Crowborough, there seems to be an accident somewhere ahead – can you give me any information?'

He was put through to the headquarters operations room. A male voice said, 'Hello, Detective Superintendent, there's a major accident. We have reports of fatalities and people trapped. The road's going to be blocked for a while – you'd be best turning around and using another route.'

Roy Grace thanked him and disconnected. Then he pulled his Blackberry from his shirt pocket, looked up Claudine's number and texted her.

She texted back almost instantly, telling him not to worry, just to get there when he could.

This made him warm to her even more.

And it helped him forget about tomorrow.

LOOKING GOOD DEAD

ONE SINGLE ACT OF KINDNESS BECOMES AN ENDLESS REIGN OF TERROR . . .

Tom Bryce did what any decent person would do. But within hours of picking up the CD that had been left behind on the train seat next to him, and attempting to return it to its owner, he is the sole witness to a vicious murder. Then his young family are threatened with their lives if he goes to the police. But supported by his wife, Kellie, he bravely makes a statement to the murder enquiry team headed by Detective Superintendent Roy Grace; a man with demons of his own to contend with.

And from that moment the killing of the Bryce family becomes a mere formality – and a grisly attraction. Notice of Kellie and Tom's deaths has already been posted on the internet. You can log on and see them on a website. They are looking good dead.

'Full of gripping twists and turns'   *Guardian*

NOT DEAD ENOUGH

THREE MURDERS. ONE SUSPECT.
NO PROOF.

On the night Brian Bishop murdered his wife he was sixty miles away, asleep in bed at the time. At least that's the way it looks to Detective Superintendent Roy Grace, who is called in to investigate the kinky slaying of beautiful socialite, Katie Bishop.

Grace soon comes to the conclusion that Bishop has performed the apparently impossible feat of being in two places at once. Has someone stolen his identity or is he simply a very clever liar? As Grace digs deeper behind the façade of the Bishops' outwardly respectable lives, it becomes clear that everything is not at all as it first seemed. Then he digs just a little too far, and suddenly the fragile stability of his own troubled, private world is facing destruction . . .

'Packed with sharp dialogue, an appealing cast and vivid cameos of the more sinister face of Brighton'   *The Times*

DEAD MAN'S FOOTSTEPS

FROM THE ASHES OF MASS DESTRUCTION . . .

Amid the tragic unfolding mayhem of the morning of 9/11, failed Brighton businessman and ne'er-do-well Ronnie Wilson sees the chance of a lifeline: to shed his debts, disappear and reinvent himself in another country. Six years later the discovery of the skeletal remains of a woman's body in a storm drain in Brighton leads Detective Superintendent Roy Grace on an enquiry spanning the globe, and into a desperate race against time to save the life of a woman being hunted down like an animal in the streets and alleys of Brighton.

'A real page-turner and the cliffhanging conclusion left me eagerly awaiting DS Grace's next outing'   *Daily Express*

'Tense, beautifully paced and excellent on police atmosphere and procedure'   *The Times*

THE WORLD STAGE PREMIERE
FROM THE NO.1 BESTSELLING AUTHOR
COMING TO A THEATRE NEAR YOU

MARRIAGE CAN BE MURDER . . .

JOSHUA ANDREWS and PETER JAMES
in association with
Paul Tyrer and Jamie Clark for
The Booking Office

PRESENT

PETER JAMES'
THE PERFECT MURDER

Featuring the young Roy Grace from
the 14 million copy crime bestseller!

Adapted by Shaun McKenna
Directed by Ian Talbot

'One of the most fiendishly clever
crime fiction plotters'
Daily Mail